HOPE IN ONE HAND...

22 SHORTS

HOPE IN ONE HAND...

22 SHORTS

PHILL BRADLEY

Dark Matter Publishing LLC

ISBN: 979-8-9916964-2-5 (eBook)
ISBN: 979-8-9916964-3-2 (Paperback)

Library of Congress Control Number: 2025908031

These stories are works of fiction. Any references to
historical events, real people, or real places are used
fictitiously. Names, characters, and places are products of
the author's imagination, and any resemblance to actual
events or persons or places, living or dead, is entirely
coincidental.

Cover design: Phill Bradley
Editing: David Yurkovich

First printing edition 2025
United States of America

Dark Matter Publishing LLC
1804 Ballinger Dr.
Spicewood, TX 78669
www.phillbradley.com

for Michelle

Contents

CONTENT ADVISORY

Some of the works in this collection contain elements of horror, violence, or death. For all stories, please expect adult violence, language, gore, and death on par with a rated R movie or MA television show. Enjoy.

PREFACE

My first collection, *Back End of the Bell Curve*, told the stories of characters down on their luck, or placed in a bad situation, and who further declined, as flawed characters are wont to do. These Schadenfreude ended on a down, or "D-minor" note, as my composer friend Craig Downie says.

In *Hope in One Hand...* I want to show that hope still lives, *especially* in dire or horrific situations, and that not everything must end badly. Reflecting on my choices, the two books could be considered a bundle with each swinging the pendulum in an extreme direction. I won't say that all the stories in this collection end well, but some do, and in all of them, the characters experience hopefulness, and sometimes even ultimate fulfillment.

In this collection, I continue to delve into the speculative fiction genre. I am fascinated by the potential of the afterlife, alien worlds, and undiscovered scientific principles. Unlike hard science fiction, which I also enjoy, speculative fiction lets you balance science and belief to find a unique middle ground. Speculative fiction also works well with the theme of hope. A lot of us believe that there is something better than what we have today, whether it is in this world or the next.

The title *Hope in One Hand...* refers to a saying that we love in Texas, but is used around the world. The line that typically follows it, "*...shit in the other and see what fills up first,*" refers to the unlikely outcome of hope pitted against what you can control or what *will* happen. The optimist in me echoes Lloyd Christmas, played by Jim Carey in the movie *Dumb and Dumber*: when Lloyd is told the chances of ending up with the girl of his dreams were one in a million, he responds, "So, you're telling me there's a chance!"

Unlike the characters in the first collection, who are weak, misguided, or taken advantage of, these characters are strong, fighting against the million-to-one odds, and (mostly) coming out victorious. Even in defeat, they have gleaned the most possible out of their situations.

As you turn the page, get ready for more stories that take place in the past, in the future, and throughout unspecified Kairos, when the events (in my view) must happen. We will visit India (twice), both American coasts, Europe, and of course, my beloved Texas. Lots of shit fills up in Texas, but we also have big hopes and big dreams. Enjoy these dreams I have put down on paper.

THIN SKIN

The extract of wild cherry bark induced quick deliveries, but Running Stream was having a difficult labor. Her legs were fatigued as she pushed and pushed, and yet the child would not fall from her; it was as if he was clinging to her insides. It was only after nightfall, as some of the elders returned from suppers, that the newborn slid from her into the arms of Forest Swallow. The blood was unimaginable.

The newborn papoose was washed and swaddled, but there was something wrong. Much of the blood was not coming from Running Stream, but from her baby boy. His skin was torn in several places: along his cheek, on both shoulders, and on his forearms. The infant was sickly-red, with prominent veins and bones.

Heart Giver, a medicine woman, hastily blessed the group. A child like this may come from the spirit world, which had a complicated relationship with their own.

The babe cried out once and then was silent. No one dared breathe until Forest Swallow indicated the child was still alive and awake, but not crying despite his numerous injuries.

Running Stream, exhausted from the ordeal, was unaware of the particulars, just that her newborn was different. She took her son and gazed into his eyes. *So large and brown like Wolf Guard's.* She remained enraptured, until his eyelids, clear as dragonfly wings, closed over the surface of his eyes, and, because of this, even as he slept, he appeared awake. Startled, she almost dropped him, then clutched him tighter. A specialness lay in his thinly-veiled, mahogany eyes. *A boy who revealed his insides through translucent skin.* He would take all the attention and training the tribe could give him to reach his potential.

Running Stream named him Leader of Peoples, but everyone called him Thin Skin. Growing up, he was prone to injury and infection. On more than one occasion he went into fever, and each time he would come out of it, stronger, and with a vision of the future: those eyes always open, always seeing, always thinking. He told tales of a great many people at war. Battling egregious enemies from other lands seemed farfetched for his peaceful tribe, but the village gathered in earnest to hear the stories and how courageous Thin Skin made his people out to be.

When he was fourteen, Thin Skin went through his rite of passage, abandoned in the wilderness with no clothing or food. The tribe's elders were split on whether or not he would survive. On the one hand, they felt he would be unable to endure the injuries commonly experienced by the young men during their induction trials, but on the other hand, he had proven more resilient than anyone expected. Coming out the other side of his fever dream, he would surely have a fantastical tale to tell. And though his skin was delicate, he was accurate with bow and spear. He was among the fastest of the boys, although his feet would be bloodied and raw after a race. His muscles were enviable, rippling right under their diaphanous covering, like so many snakes ready to be let out into the world.

One, then, two, then three days passed, and Thin Skin did not return from the forest on the other side of the great mountain. After a week, the elders went to retrieve him, if he was not yet eaten. But they returned empty-handed; he had not been found. A year elapsed. Then two.

On the eve of Thin Skin's eighteenth birthday, a distinguished man rode in on a white mustang. He was over six feet tall and dressed in foreign hides. He carried a staff made from the femur of a brown bear, and he was not alone. Twenty more warriors accompanied him. The children and women hid while the Chieftain approached the group.

"Great Chief, it is I, Leader of Peoples. I have returned to ask you, my old people, to unite with us to defend against a terrible enemy."

The chief recognized the grown man, who did not seem to blink, as the tenacious Thin Skin, with not just a tale of adventure, but adventure in action.

Thin Skin dismounted, threw down his bone staff, and knelt before the chief. He rose and then offered, "Let us go to the meeting hall. I have an incredible story to tell. And all are welcome."

The whole village assembled. Uncontrollable tears of joy ran down the face of Running Stream as her boy had come home, stronger than ever.

This Skin embraced his mother, then turned and faced the group. "During my initiation, I was sure of one thing. I would survive to lead our people. But I could not do that without knowing what I was leading them into, or away from. I knew there were others like us and not like us, but I did not know who would unite or battle. So, to find this out on my own, I made my way, leaving our village and the great mountain behind me.

"I headed north, where the snow falls every day, and met men with new ideas. They had weapons for hunting that required no skill, but were more effective than our bow and spear. They had medicines that healed my wounds and removed the pain. They had strange foods and spoke a language I did not understand.

"But they were also kind, and they allowed me to guide them through the forest and past many more mountains. They paid me with food and shelter. They had a few women and some children. I learned their language from the children, and I taught them ours.

"I found out there were many more men like this and like us. But not everyone is peaceful. Some men kill for their own benefit. The pale men told me this was one of the reasons they were traveling, to escape other bad men. To build a place where everyone is free and can raise their children in peace.

"We ran into other peoples who were like us in appearance, but not in demeanor.

"In a great battle, we were surrounded by eighty painted warriors, who would not let us pass. Our group of forty explorers was pitted against their skilled horsemen. But with our weapons and strategy, we held them off for three days. They took many casualties and were forced to allow us to continue our journey. But we could not fight unlimited battles. It was clear that if we wanted peace we would need numbers.

"My visions were right. The wars I told you about so many years ago when I was a child are true. And now the faces have names, and we must protect ourselves. There are menaces to the east and the west, and to get to each other they will pass through us.

"The men you see with me are from many different tribes and nations. We have united over 10,000 people. We will use the same strategy we used against the painted tribe to defend against and exhaust our enemies. We will protect what is ours and seek no expansion, however, we will expand by finding those of us who have a like mind and wish to live in peace.

"We are called Na'ala, the Defenders.

"So, I ask you, brothers and sisters, to unite with us, to stand up to these grievous factions, and force them to find a path to each other around us to settle their differences. I will not stay here long, but I will ask those who are willing to join our cause to defend our village and villages like ours against those who will harm us."

Ten brave men stepped forward. Then ten more, and then all. Even Running Stream and the women volunteered. And Thin Skin rejected no one. He had plans for everyone. This was how it always went for Leader of Peoples. And they built the peaceable empire, Na'ala, where all were welcome if they were willing to defend it.

As the nation grew, so did the borders, and while like-minded peoples were readily assimilated into the fold, warring tribes challenged them, attempting to overtake these territories. They often mistook Na'ala's non-aggressive behavior with timidity and met their demise attacking the unified nation. As always, Thin Skin was the tip of the spear, leading his people into combat. And he would return bloodied, but victorious, time and again.

Until they met their match against a formidable army to the west.

Pouring over the Rocky Mountains, flooding the plains and destroying everything in their path, the Wakala tribe was 100,000 strong. Scouts from Na'ala warned the outpost in time, but the tribes collided in an epic battle. For three days, the Na'ala warriors battled bravely, withdrawing only one mile in the effort to hold off the relentless surges of Wakala horsemen.

Both sides were skilled in traditional and modern weaponry, the casualties were great, and on the third day, Thin Skin, pierced by an arrow in his side, fell from his horse and was captured.

While the battle raged on, Thin Skin was brought before the Wakala general, who did not offer to negotiate. In his hubris, he believed that without their leader, the people of Na'ala would fall. He condemned Leader of Peoples to death by scalping. And in the middle of camp, bound to a wooden frame, lead warriors of the Wakala tribe took turns tearing strips from Thin Skin's body.

This Skin did not flinch or call out. It was not the first time skin had been torn from him.

The Wakala warriors became enraged. This was supposed to be a torture and a *message*. But the message was already sent. It was sent by the Leader of Peoples before the war even started. "Let me show you how to be brave, and we can all do it together."

And on that day, a frustrated Wakala army of 100,000 fell to the Na'ala tribe. And the Leader of Peoples was there to see it through rivulets of blood running over his unblinking eyes, now closed in peace.

HOTEL BLACK

There's a hotel, looking out over smooth, shiny, black boulders in a shallow bay. People go there to experience the mysterious atmosphere, to feel a calming effect from the rocks, and to die.

John and Nancy Martindale flew in on a Wednesday, with Nancy battling the last stages of terminal breast cancer. The rogue cells had metastasized six months prior, and a week ago her doctor suggested she enter hospice. He estimated she had another two weeks. John and Nancy had only had each other for the past thirty years, and John had been by her side twenty-four hours a day since she had become ill. She was not cleared for travel, but that didn't stop her. It took three flights and a ninety-minute coach ride to reach the remote hotel, and as they were ferried across the shallow inlet, first sight of the strange, floating boulders gave Nancy a feeling of fulfillment. They were magical and yet real, and the hope she had getting on the first plane, wiped out by travel fatigue, was back in the forefront. John felt a warmth as the boat passed within twenty meters of the nearest monolith, but it was probably more the pleasure on his wife's face rather than from the rock itself. She had so few victories lately.

Although most visitors assumed Hotel Black was named for the immense onyx rocks in the bay, the hotel was actually named after the founders Hugh and Christina Black, who'd started the lodging ninety-four years prior, as a getaway for wealthy families who could afford to travel. As it began with a mission to serve the most affluent, the legacy of Hotel Black was to provide superior service the wealthy class would expect.

When the Martindales arrived they were greeted by a Mr. Harrison, a spry young man of 77, whose family had served the Black estate for over eighty years. He occupied Room One, right off the lobby, allowing him to render timely assistance to the guests. The rest of the thirty-person staff resided in housing adjacent to the hotel.

Harrison welcomed the couple into the foyer of the Great Room, which was replete with vintage photographs of past patrons of the hotel and also images of the beautiful black rocks in the bay. John expected a rock to be on display in the Great Room, but none was to be seen. He said this, and Harrison explained, "The rocks remain in the bay, as they are meant to do. You may admire them from your verandah or from the grounds leading up to the bay. We have many stunning vantage points. But we never disturb the rocks. They are perfect as and where they are."

Nancy agreed, in feeble breath, saying they were "amazing," as she recalled seeing them on the short ferry ride.

"You will enjoy them tremendously during your stay here. Each time of day, and each type of weather we experience casts them in a different light, so that you may never see them the same way twice. Please," Harrison gestured in front of himself, "let me show you to your suite. You will be in Room Eleven. As you may know, we have twelve guest suites at Hotel Black, each with their own personalities, like the rocks. Suite Eleven is a beautifully appointed room and sitting room with an adjacent bathroom. Your suite has its own private balcony looking out to the bay. All of our suites are located on the floor above us, accessible by the stairway before you, or by our glass elevator next to it. Our dining room is open at 6 a.m. and will be open all day until 8 p.m. Since it is after dining room hours, we have taken the liberty of providing a selection of our cuisine in your room. Your baggage is being delivered and tipping the staff is not required or welcome, you have already paid them quite well.

"If you find you have forgotten something, please press the intercom button in your room, and my assistant, Ms. Browning, or I will answer it immediately. We will be alerted wherever we are, even in the shower!" John and Harrison laughed, and Nancy managed a wry smile and an eye squint, that said both 'Funny' and 'You scoundrel' at once.

"Shall we?" Harrison held out his hand. "After you. Let's take the lift after such a long trip." And the threesome made their way to the elevator, appreciating the way Harrison had delicately handled the obvious signs of Nancy's deteriorated health.

As they disembarked on the suite floor, they passed a younger man, sitting on a bench and mumbling to himself. "Good evening, Mister Dray," Harrison spoke to the man who neither acknowledged him, nor stopped mumbling.

"A dear fellow, that one. You will come to meet the other guests during your stay. We currently have eighteen. Mr. Dray has also come from America. He is residing in Room Seven, one of our more modern rooms. I believe we renovated it in July of 1954."

John chuckled as he and Harrison did the quick math. "Seventy-one years ago, I believe? Just like the rocks, we like to keep certain enduring aspects of the hotel."

At the door, Harrison handed them a heavy brass key with "11" inscribed on the handle. "Ever seen one of these? Original model. Give it a try."

John expertly manipulated the key in the loose lock and the door swung inward.

"I will leave you to retire, and see you at the morning breakfast, if you so choose." And with a slight bow, Harrison left John and Nancy Martindale at the threshold of the impeccable room at Hotel Black.

Nancy felt like a little girl again, spoiled with a bedroom fit for a queen: a pillowy bed, not too high or too low, and a buffet of foods she probably wouldn't eat, but was appreciative to have offered to her. John opened the slatted French doors that led out to the balcony. Nancy joined him, and as they peered outwards toward the bay, they took in the moonlight reflecting off the rocks' surfaces, lighting up the whole bay and parts of the bank beyond. From this vantage, they counted at least twenty of the massive domes, although the number was twice that, past the point of visibility to the left or right.

John put his arm around Nancy's shoulders, and she put her arm around his waist, and they were not sad. They were exactly where they were supposed to be.

The night passed quickly and uneventfully in the comfortable bed. In the morning, John checked to ensure Nancy was still breathing and snuck out to the balcony. Whispered voices came from a few balconies to the left, but privacy dividers blocked the guests. *Must be around Room Eight or Nine*, he thought. Birds chittered, but he didn't spot any roosting on the black rocks that now reflected early sunshine from just above the eastern horizon, blindingly bright off the shiny surfaces. The water coruscated around the base of the boulders as if carrying diamonds or crystal. He had expected it to be brackish, as the rocks blocked a natural flow. Now, in daylight, the monoliths extended far to the east and the west, and John wondered if there were more around these parts or if they were only near Hotel Black.

Nancy was struggling with the door to the verandah, and John opened it for her. She looked better than she had in a while, though he had heard cancer patients sometimes have the best days just before they pass on. Still, she was in good spirits as he helped her onto the wooden deck. "I heard our neighbors a few doors down," motioning to the left. "Seems the thing to do... look at the rocks."

"They're fascinating, aren't they? Each slightly different and beautiful in its own way."

"Yes, they are. And so are you." He kissed her tenderly. "You slept all night. Do you feel better? Would you like to try some breakfast this morning?"

"I can tag along with you, maybe peck at a scone. Or have some hot coffee." Even Nancy would have to be hungry after not eating any of the delicacies in their room the previous evening. John had not passed up the opportunity. The six-foot-four, 280-pound former athlete had sampled the fare enough for both travelers.

They made their way toward the dining room and met up with a couple coming out of Room Eight who introduced themselves as the Winters, Mark and Evelyn. John asked if they had been on the balcony that morning, and they confirmed. They also said that something strange had happened to Colby Dray, their next-door neighbor. They think he fell over the side of his terrace, but when they went to look, they didn't see anything in the bushes below. It was too late to go knocking to determine if he was okay, but hopefully Mr. Harrison would know something at breakfast.

When they reached the dining room, Mr. Harrison welcomed them again and introduced Ms. Browning, a woman of about forty, wearing a long plaid skirt and a neat blouse, and sporting fashionable glasses. John thought she looked like a sexy librarian. Nancy knew what John was thinking and elbowed his waist.

"You look lovely Mrs. Martindale; you must have slept well."

"Yes, very well."

"And the room? It's to your liking?"

"Oh, it's wonderful. I felt like Cinderella."

"I hope it was the princess version and not the maid version."

"Yes, Mr. Harrison," and she blushed a little. He was so debonair, and his sense of humor was so personable.

"I see you are with Mr. and Mrs. Winters from Room Eight. Will you be dining together?"

They looked around at each and other and simultaneously consented.

They selected a table and Evelyn pulled Mr. Harrison aside. "Is everything okay with Colby Dray? We heard some commotion on his balcony and then nothing. We were concerned he fell over, but when we looked, he was gone."

Mr. Harrison was transparent. "What you suspected did happen. Mr. Dray *did* have an accident last night, but I assure you he is just fine. In fact, he returned to his room early this morning, and should be joining us later in the day."

Evelyn decided to let it go and joined the others where she recounted what Harrison had told her. "Do you think maybe it wasn't an accident? That he tried... to *harm* himself?"

"He's definitely got some issues," John chimed in, digging into a second custard, "and I've only seen him for less than a minute."

Evelyn lowered her voice even more. "They say some people come here *to die*. I wonder if he was one of those people."

Nancy bit her tongue. She didn't dare bring up her end goal in front of judgy Evelyn, but she also thought she should say something. "I've heard that. Something about the rocks helps people to come to terms with life and death."

"Well, I, for one, think they are just to die *for*," Evelyn tittered at her own joke. Everyone else acknowledged her cleverness with awkward smiles.

They enjoyed their poached salmon and roasted potatoes, ending with a mini-soufflé. All the meals at Hotel Black were well-prepared and delicious. Even Nancy found enough appetite to sample everything.

Mark and Evelyn invited the Martindales for an afternoon hike, but John made up an excuse: they needed to tend to some family business. "Maybe we will see you at dinner."

"*Ciao*," said the bubbly Evelyn as they went their separate ways.

On the way back from lunch, the door was ajar for Suite Nine, the one with Colby Dray, but as they passed, it shut quickly, giving them a start. "I guess he's okay…. Back in the room," deduced John.

"Best we steer clear of him," Nancy proclaimed, although she reasoned he was more of a harm to himself than to the other guests. And what if he was somehow dangerous? She was a stone's throw away from the tomb anyway. "On the other hand…" she stopped, walked back to the door, and knocked. There was no answer, but she could hear heavy breathing on the other side of the door. She called out to Colby in a soothing voice, "I'm glad you're okay, Colby. Get some rest." She rejoined her surprised husband. "The boy needs something encouraging in his life, John."

Late in the day, after a nap in the clean, white sheets of the very comfortable bed, John and Nancy gazed out at the rocks from their balcony. Other visitors to the hotel were milling about, near the bank of the bay, taking in a close-up view and enjoying each other's company.

"Isn't this peaceful, John? This is where I want to spend my last days. Not in some hospital. Here with you, in this perfect place."

John said nothing. That was part of being a supportive spouse. He didn't like the talk of Nancy's imminent demise, but facing it on her own terms was important to her, and thus, important to him.

Changing the subject, he announced, "Let's get ready for dinner!"

"Oh, John, I think every pound I lose goes straight to you." And they laughed as they made for the shower and the dressing room, putting on the best clothes they had worn in years.

At dinner, they were paired with a different couple, William and Helene Lockett, from Bradford, England. They were not shy about why they had come to Hotel Black. Helene explained William had advanced heart disease and wanted one last trip before succumbing to it. William, in a wheezy voice said, "My ankles are swollen; I can't breathe right; I could go at any time. Might as well be here instead of that dreary city."

Having something in common with William, Nancy wished to confide in the Locketts, but she still wasn't certain if anyone besides John should know. Maybe it was the way Evelyn had said, "...come here *to die,*" that made the subject taboo.

Surprisingly, Colby Dray showed up at dinner, and most unsurprisingly, sat by himself at the furthest table in the small dining area. There was audible murmuring at the other tables. Nancy was sure Evelyn had spilled the beans about Colby's "issue" to some of the other guests.

Colby acknowledged Nancy with a glance, which said, "Thanks for stopping by, but you can't help me. No one can." One of the younger waitresses attended to Colby with the utmost dignity, which is the way all the staff treated the visitors to Hotel Black.

The Martindales and Locketts had barely started their main course when Colby left, after having eaten only a small soup and a roll. Nancy wanted to go after him, but John reached over and put his hand on her forearm, and, without looking at her, quietly suggested in her ear, "Give the boy his space."

The evening was spent by the guests relaxing in the Great Room and walking around the well-lit property, as one of the butlers expertly played on the baby grand near the staircase. Nancy and John met several other travelers, some of whom may have been carrying burdens such as Nancy's, and others who seemed fit, just interested in the mysterious black rocks and the history of the hotel.

They learned that Mr. Harrison had grown up here, his mother tending the books and his father keeping the grounds. When Ann Black, the only child of Hugh and Christina, passed, it turned out she had bequeathed the entire estate to Harrison. He had been her constant companion throughout her life, except for a few years at the University in her youth. It was a fascinating place, the Hotel Black, and, the Martindales guessed, full of fascinating stories.

The next morning, as the Martindales strolled the corridor toward a late brunch, the maids were turning over Colby's room, and in the dining hall, Nancy asked Mr. Harrison what happened to him.

"Oh, he had an early checkout, Mrs. Martindale. His time to stay with us was over."

It didn't sit well with her that Colby's appearances and disappearances were so mysterious, but she just said, "I hope he gets the help he needs. I think he's misunderstood."

"All of us are a little misunderstood, sometimes," replied Harrison. "It's nice to keep him in your thoughts. Now how about some of Mrs. Potsdam's famous German pancake?"

"Oh yeah," said John. "With a scoop of - no, *two scoops* of—ice cream."

"A strong appetite, that one," he said to Nancy.

"He's eating for two," she said and poked John's generous waistline.

After brunch, the Martindales chose to try the five-minute hike to the bay to examine the black rocks up close. In fact, Nancy was the most energetic she had been in three or four months. They took the well-manicured path through the heather and listened to the crickets sing. Other visitors meandered near the bay shoreline, some of them even in the water, though only to their shins, all keeping a safe distance from the rocks.

At that proximity, the onyx stones were colossal, several times the size of an automobile, and extremely smooth, as if polished by giants. The water in the bay flowed slowly, but deliberately, from east to west, around the great boulders, continuing to polish their sides. The sheen on the rocks above the waterline indicated that, at one time, water may have covered this whole area. Now, the inlet was no more than six feet deep in most areas; John could clearly see the bottom, made up of pebbles and sand. Oddly, no vegetation grew in the water around the rocks, despite the conditions probably being ideal for the lush bank to seed the shallow basin under the ample light penetrating through to the bay floor. The disharmony made John uneasy, as if the rocks had some power over life and death.

Along the shoreline the hotel had placed benches with dedications on them. John and Nancy sat on a bench dedicated to Ann Black that seemed to have *the* prime view. "Excellent choice, Nancy. She loved this spot." Mr. Harrison was right behind them. He apologized. "Sorry to startle you. This is where I come when I need a break. I miss Ann very much. When she was alive, we used to sit here and talk and play a game called, 'Up to Three.' It's like paper, scissors, rock but with points. Nancy, would you like to play? It's very simple. Two beats one. Three beats two, and one beats three. "If you win, you get how many points you choose. First one to ten wins the game."

Nancy loved games and couldn't resist. Harrison counted to three, and they showed their fingers. Nancy chose two. Harrison also. Minutes later, Nancy won, ten to eight.

Harrison shook her hand. "Good match. I have to get back to the hotel, but it was a pleasure playing the game with you."

Nancy's eyes sparkled like the water in the river, and she wished they could play again. She and John could play, but Nancy felt it wouldn't be the same. John had always been such a fuddy-duddy about games.

The Martindales spent their remaining days at Hotel Black meeting guests, playing "Up to Three" with Harrison, and spending quality time together. It felt like a second honeymoon, not the final destination she had expected it to be.

After dinner on their last day, Nancy said, "John, let's take the stairs." And though the last few steps were difficult, she made it to the top and gave herself a little fist pump like she had conquered Everest.

Nancy took a moment to peruse the old portraits and photos from the hotel's history. In one, a man who looked like Mr. Harrison was welcoming a hotel guest. She thought it was Harrison's father, but below, a caption said, "Mr. Black welcomes Winston Churchill to the Hotel."

Nancy was confused by the striking resemblance and then had a thought. In the room, she confided in John. "I think Mr. Harrison might be Mr. Black's son. They look identical. And he was born soon after his family started working here. And why would the Blacks bequeath the hotel to him?"

John couldn't argue. Nancy had a nose for that sort of thing. "Maybe that's why he and Ann were just friends…."

"Hmmm. This place is even more interesting than I thought. We might need to stay an extra week. I certainly don't feel like I'm going to die anytime soon."

John had to agree. If this is where people came to die, the atmosphere and hospitality made it difficult to close the deal. And one more week with Nancy like this would mean the world to him. "I'll talk to Harrison in the morning."

"I'm afraid it's just not possible, Mr. Martindale. We have guests coming in tonight for Room Eleven, and we have no other vacancies. But you *are* welcome to rebook. As it happens, we have a cancellation for next week. You *could* spend a few days in a nearby town and then rejoin us."

John read Nancy's disappointment mixed with hope. "We'll take it."

As the coach pulled up to take them to the ferry, Nancy went over to Harrison and gave him a big hug. "Thanks for everything. I will see *you* in *two* days," and held up two fingers, her last winning hand.

As they pulled away, Hugh Harrison Black wiped away a tear. He did not expect to see Nancy again. No one had *ever* died at Hotel Black, but out there, past the beautiful, black rocks, they were on their own.

FINDING COMFORT

Lydia and Elmer played at the edge of the forest. Mom said it would be okay as long as she could see them from the window. As young children, they'd chase the butterflies that would dart in and out of the copse. Watching in wonder as the beautiful insects landed on the phlox, they'd coax them up onto their little fingers, holding their breath and hoping to not startle the delicate creatures.

All the insects of the forest held a fascination for the twins, who, unlike other children, preferred each other's company and the company of the forest critters to classmates. Mom and Dad saw no issue with their children's hobby. It was comforting to have them grow up close by without the distractions and antics typical of the children in town.

When the youngsters learned that butterflies came from caterpillars, they would search the bark of nearby trees to find them and nurse them until it was time to pupate. They asked Dad for nets to drape over the tree limbs to prevent birds from feeding on the chrysalides.

Lydia and Elmer didn't like birds and treated them all like insectivores. For their seventh birthdays, as they requested, the twins received slingshots and defended against anything that threatened the grove. They'd leave the dead birds on the ground for the ants and beetles to feed on. The flies would lay their eggs and eventually have babies, "maggots" as Mom called them. Maggots would get their wings also, just like butterflies.

Mom had a strict rule of keeping insects out of the house. But sometimes, at night, the kids longed for their pals. They didn't realize it, but they had formed a bond with the creatures. For so long they aimed to nurture and comfort the small beings, but over time, they became emotionally dependent on the comfort the animals provided *them*. So their mother's rule was broken as tiny companions were smuggled into the house. Elmer needed to feel earthworms writhing in his hand before he could fall asleep. Lydia liked the feeling of centipedes crawling on her palm, trying to understand the cadence of their many, many feet, like a code only she could one day break.

Mom would discover the little beasts when she went to strip the sheets, or Dad would detect something scuttling out of the corner of his eye while he watched the football game, but they never said anything, disposing of the bugs quietly and efficiently.

When the twins were fifteen, Mom relaxed the rule and let Elmer keep a giant walking stick, named Brice. As long as Brice was kept in a terrarium, in Elmer's room, he was allowed in the house. But she often found Brice in her bathroom, or on the blinds, or near the kitchen sink. She was sick of Brice not being in the terrarium, so she locked the skinny bug in the basement until Elmer could prove to be more responsible. She warned Elmer that if he didn't keep Brice in his habitat, she would release him back into the forest.

Try as he may, Elmer was unable to maintain control of Brice, and one day Mom made good on her word, releasing Brice back into the wild. Sixteen-year-old Elmer had a mental breakdown and stopped communicating. Lydia tried to tell her mom that Elmer needed Brice to cope with life.

But Mom, as patient, and kind, and understanding as she was, could not fathom such a concept. She told Lydia that life was uncomfortable, and Elmer would do better to get used to it.

During this time, Lydia continued to smuggle her centipedes into the house undetected. After hearing Mom's take on pets, Lydia, afraid for her brood, went to great lengths to hide them while she was away from the house. One morning, when Lydia was at school, Mom stretched to replace an old photo album on the high shelf in Lydia's closet when she accidentally tipped the stack of boxes. Out rained a hundred centipedes into Mom's hair and down her blouse. She passed out from fright, and that's where Elmer found her.

When Lydia returned home, Mom had still not awakened, and, knowing they were both in trouble, they grabbed as many pets as possible, their sleeping bags, and headed to the forest.

Dad arrived home to find his wife groggy but alive, and no sign of the twins. They first checked the edge of the forest, and then called the sheriff. Although the twins never ventured deep into the woods, usually staying along the tree line, it was most likely that's where they were.

Even with the police they couldn't make much progress during the night, but in the morning, they discovered the twins about a quarter-mile into the thicket. Lydia was in anaphylactic shock. Her airway had become blocked and required an emergency tracheotomy. Her eyes fluttered as she lost consciousness, and she was hospitalized in a comatose state.

Though Elmer remained uncommunicative, rocking back and forth in the hospital room's chair, the doctors and sheriff had a pretty good idea of what had occurred. Lydia's sleeping bag had several crushed centipedes, and she had bite marks all over her body. They surmised the bugs crawled into her sleeping bag at night, looking for food. But her parents knew Lydia had deliberately placed them there, zipping the bag up tight, to keep them in.

After a couple of days, the tracheostomy was reversed. Lydia started breathing on her own, but she remained hospitalized and unresponsive. Elmer, sad for himself and for Lydia, snuck out of the house in the middle of the night to visit her. But he was not alone. With him, he brought a large centipede from the forest, Lydia's favorite type. Undetected, he entered her room and placed the creature in her upturned palm, where it scurried up her arm into her gown. He tracked the movement of the animal, catching it time and again as it exited her loose clothing, re-placing it in her palm, and letting it re-roam her body. And Lydia started to move her mouth. She was learning the centipede's code and learning to live again.

At 5 a.m., the duty nurse, making her rounds, spotted Elmer, but before she could tell him visiting hours weren't until nine, she noticed an awake and blinking Lydia holding a long insect in her hand. Alarmed, the nurse tried to swat the bug away, but Lydia hid the animal in her gown. Not able to take on Elmer and Lydia herself, she ran for help.

Lydia made a full recovery and her parents understood it was due to the centipede. *Maybe*, they thought, *they had gone too far to ban the creatures from their children's lives.*

Upon arriving home as a complete family, Elmer was allowed another walking stick. He began to communicate again, named it Franklin, and cared for it with the utmost responsibility.

Though Mom and Dad were still creeped out by the centipedes, Lydia proved capable of keeping them out of the rest of the house and was permitted to keep four. As long as they were kept fed, she was allowed to handle them. And they roamed her body tapping out the code, providing the critical comfort she craved.

HOPPERS OF HOPPERS

"Hey there, little fella," Homer Freer called out to the grasshopper that landed on the wooden table near his beer. The insect looked up at him and then rotated to also take in the farmland beyond.

Homer welcomed the company, watching the sun set from the comfort of his porch after a long day in the field. His wife, Mabel, was inside prepping dinner: roasted potatoes and corn and a re-heat of the chicken they didn't finish the night before. The Freers had needed to make meals stretch. The upcoming crop would be a good one, but they didn't have much saved from the recent lean years. President Grant's policies hadn't helped the farmers.

As dusk fell, Homer got up and told the small green bug, "I gotta get. Help yourself to the barley." As if he understood, the creature took flight out into the swaying fields.

The next morning, as usual, Homer awoke at dawn, donned his trousers and shirt, and made some strong coffee. The house was still dim. "Didn't expect no rain today," he said as he strode to the door.

The skies were overcast, alright. But not with rain clouds, with hordes of flying insects. Locusts. Millions of them descending onto the farm. On the windows, on the porch, and most certainly feasting in the field. Homer turned back inside before too many found their way through the threshold, dozens of them clinging to the cuffs of his shirt and filling the brim of his hat.

After killing the unwelcome visitors, he woke Mabel. Homer and Mabel had been around for the locust plague of 1856, which devastated that year's crops, and this one looked just as bad, or worse, judging from the darkened skies. They'd have to hunker down, maybe a week or more, and they were overdue for a trip to town. The cupboard was bare, and the two-hour drive to Fleming had been postponed to take advantage of the pleasant weather the past few days.

Forty acres of barley were only weeks from harvest. Homer sat with his head in his hands not sure what to do. They would be on rations a full 'nother year.

Midway through the day, with no sign of abatement, came a frantic knock on the door. Grady, the Black fella from down the way, had braved the plague with a small gristmill in his hand.

Grady Franklin was the nicest and most positive person Homer had ever met, and the Freers hustled him inside with minimal invasion from the buzzing critters. Grady told them that if they wanted to work together, he might have a plan to reclaim some of their lost revenue.

"You see, Homer. These green bugs are like green*backs* down south. You can *eat* 'em, and they're really good for ya, but ya can't never catch enough."

Homer and Mabel looked at each other like Grady had gone off his nut. But Grady explained that if you caught enough locusts and ground them down into meal, you could make lots of tasty dishes with them. "If you add plenty of pepper or salt, or maybe some sage. It might not catch on 'round here, but you could sell it in the South for a pretty penny." He told the Freers he just needed some nets and such to prove it to them.

Well, Homer and Mabel figgered they had to be pretty hungry to eat a bug and told Grady so, but Grady went over to the window and smashed one of the invaders. He picked off the back legs and popped the rest in his mouth and ate it right there in front of the bewildered Freers.

After making a funny face, Grady perked back up. "Can I get a glass o' water? They don't have much taste, but they awfully dry."

Mabel poured him a glass, still looking at him as if he wasn't the man they knew before.

"I don't know what you're doing there, Grady, but I don't think this is the business for us." Homer wasn't sure of his next move. but was almost certain this wasn't it.

"Look, here Homer. How 'bout I make you some tasty muffins with the locust meal, and then you can decide? Ah, but if you're too scared to eat 'em, we can still talk about what we can do. I heard you had some nets you got way back after the '56 invasion. I say we use them nets. It's too late to keep 'em out, so.. let's keep 'em in. You help me net 'em and process 'em and I'll do all the sellin'."

"Grady, them nets are in the barn all piled up. You can help yourself, but I'm not sure I'm your man."

"I always liked you folks." And Grady tipped his hat as he let himself out into the onslaught, walking through the throng of bugs as if he didn't have a care in the world. Later, they saw him stretching the nets over vast surfaces of grain, grabbing the corners, and reeling in hundreds of thousands of locusts.

On day three, seeing how devoted he was, and having nothing better to do, Homer joined him. The two men started a sulfur fire in the clearing to kill the netted pests by smoking them. They dumped the creatures in an empty grain hopper and over the next week it filled to ten feet.

Grady made some of his sage muffins in the kitchen, but Mabel wasn't keen on it. She told Grady to keep any utensils that touched the creatures, but she did grant that the muffins smelled pretty good. On day five, Homer ate one and was surprised that it wasn't awful. He wasn't about to tell Mabel that Grady's locust muffins were better than hers, so he kept it to himself, but he was starting to see Grady's vision.

For three weeks they harvested locusts every day. Homer did it just thinking it was something to do, still not bought in on the commercial viability of the bugs. They set up smokers all around the perimeter of the farm, and Homer was surprised, having been through the '56 plague that new swarms continued to arrive, but they did so only to be suffocated and die on the Freer premises.

After four weeks, the locusts moved on. The main crop was destroyed, but the new product was ready to be processed. Grady took over, finding a mill in St. Louis to handle the grinding and tinning.

The first can of Franklin and Freer locust meal rolled off the line two weeks later. The cans went for one dollar and fifty cents and sold like hotcakes. After all, you could make hotcakes. Delicious ones, with a pinch of sage.

FISHPLACE

It was our twenty-third anniversary. Anne and I went down to Cozumel for a relaxing vacation. We had nothing planned but to play at the hotel, sit by the pool, tan on the beach, and have a few romantic meals.

On our third day, Anne decided to try the open-air Fish Spa down on the beach, right by the water's edge. The day before, we met a honeymooning couple in the open-air hut, having a pedicure by dipping their feet into a well of live fish. The small fish, called Garra Rufas, or Doctor fish, suck the dead skin off your feet, while you relax and gaze out at the beautiful ocean. It's supposed to be a painless treatment; the brightly colored and toothless fish are only two inches long. Several hundred of them patrolled the well, and the couple we talked to said the fish tickled a bit, but otherwise, it was just relaxing.

"Looks like fun, Stephen," Anne jibed me, as she made a little fish face and tickled my side.

"Not for me, babe. But go ahead knock yourself out. Just hope the little fellas don't choke on your bunions."

"I don't have bunions, honey. I have cute little girl feet." She wasn't wrong; they were perfect.

"Well fine. You can have your feet sucked on by the fish, and I will suck on them later after you take a shower."

"Naughty boy," she scolded, but didn't mean it, as she playfully poked me in the rib.

After checking in Anne for the forty-five-minute session at the spa, I stuck around for the first couple of minutes to see if she'd really like it. The spa lady gave her a set of high-end wireless headphones, and she got to pick the music, which was, of course, early 2000's bangers: Katy Perry, Britney Spears, Beyonce, et cetera.

Anne was bopping her head from side to side as the fish started nibbling away. She was lost in her world, and I struggled to get her attention, giving her a questioning thumbs-up sign. She replied, "It's awesome!" about twenty decibels too loud. The spa lady and I laughed, and I went back to the hotel room to read a book in air-conditioned comfort .

When I got to our room, I threw my wallet, the hotel key, and my phone onto the bed. I looked around and couldn't find my book until I remembered I left it on the balcony the day before. I grabbed a beer from the minibar and went out on the balcony to retrieve my book, which had blown off the table.

The night before was so calm, but now the palm trees up and down the beach leaned and the flags flapped noisily in the courtyard below.

Even from the fourteenth floor, I could see the fish place and Anne's head bobbing to the music. I turned around, thinking, "She's so crazy," and went to reopen the balcony door, but it wouldn't open. The stupid stick they used as a locking mechanism had fallen down into the track and was, well, doing its job.

So much for the air-conditioned book-read. But there were plenty of worse places to be than drinking a beer and reading a book on a balcony overlooking a beautiful beach, with palm trees hypnotically swaying to the surf. Or so I thought.

I had only read about three pages when I heard shouting and screaming coming from the beach.

My first thought was Anne...*something wrong had happened with the fish...* but the reality was much worse.

People on the grounds near the hotel were being attacked by, I don't know... *marauders*? That's the word that came to mind when I saw about a dozen guys brandishing machetes, attacking the guests, accosting them for their phones and jewelry. Several patrons were already down on the ground, bleeding, maybe dead, and others were running, in all directions. Anne, oblivious to the commotion, was merrily vibing to her playlist at the spa.

The spa and restaurant workers hunkered down in the cabana about sixty feet from her and were trying to get her attention without alarming the terrorists, but to no avail, which wasn't surprising. I had trouble getting her attention earlier from only five feet away.

The bandits fanned out to catch the stragglers, and any runaways who were overtaken were struck down and slashed. Some of the patrons were fleeing into the ocean, to the left, out of the line of sight for Anne, who maybe had her eyes shut anyway. A few of them were nabbed in the shallow surf, but the rogues didn't seem to be venturing out to attack runners already over waist-deep.

My phone was on the other side of the glass door so I couldn't call 911, if 911 was even appropriate in Mexico. I shouted down the row of balconies. Other guests were on their phones, but surely by the time the federales arrived, there would be no one left, except those far out in the ocean.

I had to do something to save Anne. I grabbed the balcony chair, which was metal, and tried smashing through the glass window, which was very resistant. Too resistant. However, a tiny crack had formed, and I put my heel into it, shattering the whole door.

I peered over the balcony once more to see that one of the marauders had split off from the others and was heading toward the cabana and Anne's spa deck. The cabana employees were funneling around the side and out toward the neighboring resort, leaving Anne completely unprotected, except for one young man who remained hidden with his eyes on Anne and her would-be attacker.

I grabbed the biggest shard of glass I could find and headed down the stairs, blind with rage, wanting to protect Anne, but not sure what my plan would be. My only hope was that the police would arrive soon, otherwise I had to try to lure the lone bandit away from Anne and toward me. When I burst into the lobby, hotel security was manning the rear resort doors, barring the patrons from the beach.

"My wife's out there!" I screamed at the men blocking the exit.

"*Señor*, *la policia* are coming. You must stay in here."

"She's at the fishplace!" I pointed toward the spa and the vandal headed in that direction. "He's going to kill her! Let me out!" The manager sighed, reluctantly unlocking the door for me, and doing the sign of the cross as I blasted past him. I ran across the patio and onto the sand screaming at the guy in black, but the strong winds took my voice off to the right.

He had now spotted Anne and her bright red headphones at the spa and was headed her way. I don't know what he wanted with a defenseless woman, but he was definitely curious, fixated on her, and now only about thirty feet from the spa.

I was easily five times that distance from him, shouting the whole time, but he couldn't hear me, just as Anne couldn't hear him. The rest of his crew was escaping farther down the beach to the left. I had blurred them out, and the people in the ocean, and at that moment there was only the three of us in the entire world.

He was only a few feet behind Anne as she obliviously stretched and started to dance from the waist up. And that's when he stopped, machete in hand, and did a little dance of his own behind her, shaking his hips as if he was dancing along with her.

I don't know if he felt invincible, was mocking her, or was in his own private world with my beautiful wife, but he still hadn't sensed me coming up behind him. I had closed the gap to fifty feet, still shouting at him, and finally, he turned to face me, alarmed as I broke his trance.

However, seeing me standing there with a shard of glass the size of a pineapple slice must have been amusing, because he smiled and launched toward *me*, taking the bait. He was a lot faster on the sand than I expected. I spun and ran to the right, toward the next property down the beach where the workers had fled from the cabana.

I thought I was in good shape, but he was closing the gap. From my current position, I couldn't reach the ocean, and I wasn't so sure he wouldn't follow me there even if I could. My only hope was to get to some solid ground and pick up speed. Get to help.

But there was no path, no people, just slow, slow sand. He was now close behind me, yelling something in super-fast Spanish, and I knew he would overtake me in the next fifteen seconds. I looked over my shoulder, and that's when he fell. I did a mental sign of the cross and kept running, looking back after about thirty seconds, to see that he had still not gotten up.

I stopped, my heart rate through the roof from fear and the extreme cardio workout.

The young man from the cabana was walking with a revolver, still pointed at the bandit, and a couple hundred feet back stood Anne, alone, crying as she took note of the carnage on the beach and the patio.

The cabana guy arrived at the marauder, but there was no movement, his first shot had been true. The federales and medical personnel were now storming the beach, trying to save what lives were left. I ran back toward Anne, passing the young man with the revolver, thanking him for saving my life and Anne's, knowing he hung back to protect her.

Anne and I ran into each other's arms, saying nothing, but taking comfort in our continued existence. An EMT woman placed a blanket around us and sat us down on the side of the fish tank, while she bandaged my hand, which, unbeknownst to me, was bleeding profusely from clutching the glass shard.

Later, I had to give a statement, as did Anne, who said she saw nothing but the shot that killed the final raider. The man from the cabana, licensed through hotel security to carry a gun, was named Tiburón, which means "shark" in Spanish.

My Anne, strong as ever, decided that she was never in danger, protected by both kinds of fish on the beach. And after we returned to Dallas, she got tattoos of the Garra Rufas swimming around her left ankle and a *tiburón* arched around her right.

TUNNELS IN 2D

I grew up in a traditional Los Angeles home. My dad was a tattoo artist, and Mom was a maid at a run-down motel named the Four Seasonz. We lived in El Segundo near the beach, and I had a pretty good childhood, by which I mean, my parents never let me starve and told me school was important, probably in hopes that I would find better jobs than they had, and come back and support them. My parents didn't do drugs, which I thought was hard for them, based on what I saw from some of our neighbors. They drank a little, but I wouldn't say excessively. They loved me, and I loved them.

Despite my dad and mom being inked, I wasn't into tattoos. You know how they say each generation rebels against the one before? Well, I preferred to keep my clean, surfer look.

In high school, I spent a lot of time hanging out at Dockweiler, which is one of the closest and coolest beaches near us. I'd just bum a ride after school, or on weekends I'd walk there and hang out all day with my friends.

By the time I graduated, I was about six-three, and only about 150 pounds soaking wet. I had washboard abs and a tiny twenty-six inch waist. They called me 2D, because from the side I had no real width from front to back.

One night, about a week after graduation, I was hanging out with my bros, Matt and Jonas, and a coupla chicks from school. We had a bonfire going on the beach, and Matt was showing us his new brow piercing. Jonas also had piercings, as well as tunnels in his earlobes. He'd started about three years ago when he was only sixteen and they were, by then, about the size of a quarter.

Some of my dad's friends and clients also had stretched earlobes. They said it was traditional, but to me, an adopted tradition isn't the same thing as a cultural tradition. Like those old white guys with the tribal tattoo around their bicep. I mean, what tribe do *you* belong to? Realistically, it's just a cool design; you don't have to justify it. I think people do that stuff for lots of reasons, some being personal, some being superficial, but what people do to their bodies should be their choice no matter what the reason.

"Nice metal, bra. It sets off your eyes," Jonas joked to Matt.

"Fuck you, dude," Matt replied, whipping his head back to get his bangs out of his eyes, smiling from the hit he'd just taken.

"2D, when you gonna get pretty like me?" Jonas teased, and flicked his earlobe.

"No one could be as pretty as you," I deflected. Again. They knew I was anti-tattoo, anti-bodimod.

Jonas said something to Matt and Matt laughed his ass off. "Dude, there's probably only three inches from your belly button to your back. We could totally do it."

"Do what?"

"I bet we could pierce you right through your whole bod."

"What would be the point of that?"

Jonas shrugged. "I guess you'd be the first person to do it. That'd be *wicked*."

Matt added. "If anyone could do it, man, it'd be you, 2D."

I told them both to fuck off, but when I got home, I decided to check it out on the internet to see if it was even possible.

There seemed to be some serious challenges to this plan, even if it was only three inches. First of all, there were abs to go through: piercing muscle would be a lot different from piercing skin or cartilage.

I know from my mom that when she got her tongue pierced, they did it in the middle between the two tongue muscles to avoid the veins underneath, and the internet said the abs also have connecting tissue between them called the Linea Alba. I called it the LA because I'm from LA, and it helped me remember it. You could totally pierce the LA and not get hurt.

And then there were intestines. Even though I was skinny, I could tell my guts were down there. Once we went to Shakey's in Inglewood, and I ate fourteen slices, and the next day my gut was like I had a boa constrictor in there. It was all squiggly and fat.

Besides my abs, intestine, and colon, there was the appendix on the right side (which for me had been taken out at age eleven) and of course the spine down the middle, which seemed like a total dealbreaker.

I thought my kidneys would be in the way also, but to my surprise, they were way higher up. When my friends and I used to pretend to kidney punch each other, we punched just above our butts. Turns out we'd been way off.

For some reason, I felt like it was something I had to try, like, *maybe I could do it.* Go through the LA between my abs, miss some intestines, then go out through either side of my back and avoid the spine. But it would be crooked, not symmetrical. In the middle of the night, it hit me. I could do *two* tunnels, make a loop around the spine and come back through the other side and then back through the starting point, and it *would* be symmetrical.

I sketched it on a pad of paper and showed it to my friends.

"That's radical, dude." Jonas was totally tripping out on my sketch.

"Ditto," agreed Matt. "But who would do such an epic piercing? You gotta go to a doctor. It's not like your mom could do it."

Jonas, ever helpful, said, "I know this guy Mario who said he knows a guy who is a doctor for some gang, and he removes bullets outside of a real hospital. Maybe he'd do it."

It turned out Mario didn't know shit. He knew someone who knew someone else who knew a rumor about a doctor. We kept asking around, and finally, we found this guy named Fernando Peña who used to be one in Colombia but couldn't practice here in the US.

I had to leave a message with this gang banger from my old government class and got approached two days later for a meet-up at OB's in Manhattan Beach.

Inside, there was only one old Colombian-looking dude, and when I walked up, he said, "TooDee? I'm Peña. You want food? I'm buying."

I said I'd take a Coke Zero. And rings.

The waitress got our order, and he continued. "Lemme get these right…" he said in his Colombian, now South-LA accent. "You say you want a hole? All the way through… your body?" and made a fist and stuck his index finger into it, looking up at me above his glasses to check for understanding.

I pulled out the sketch from my pocket and showed him. I had added a couple of new views: a cutaway, a side view, a front view, and a back view to go along with the original line drawing.

"Oh…," he paused trying to take it all in. "These would be very difficult. So many nerves. And muscle in the back."

I hadn't considered the lower back muscles. *Damn.*

He explained that the lower back connects the glutes to the lats right where I wanted to go. Penetrating this would weaken the lower back, and I'd lose mobility and likely have severe chronic back pain. It was a no-go.

"Hmmm, but perhaps…"

"Perhaps, what?" I said and noticed I had already eaten all my rings.

"Maybe it's possible to come out by the Lumbar Triangle…," and he got a pen from this shirt pocket. "May I?"

I motioned for him to mark up my drawings as needed. He pointed to an area about an inch or two away from the spine, which didn't change the design that much.

Then he asked, "Why you want these big loop to connect them? Maybe... jus' make the tunnels, here... and here, like so..." And he drew two dotted-line cylinders through the body just like the tunnels in Josh's ears. "And first we make the hole small, but then we make it bigger. Like those fools with the rings in their earlobes." Now he was catching my drift.

I chimed in. "Right. Like only twenty gauge to start. Really small." And I made a circle with my thumb and forefinger as if we were agreeing on the precise size. Then stretch it out over time."

Fernando slapped the table. "By God, let's do it! It will cost you about... hmmm... forty."

I wasn't sure what he was saying, but I guessed. "Forty thousand dollars?"

"*Si, compadre*. What else? Forty blowjobs? Ha ha ha."

I told him, "I don't even have forty dollars. I mean... I'm just a kid."

"Well, keed, you gotta have forty thousand dollars, or I can't do it. The anesthesia, the skin graft. It's gonna cost real *dinero*."

Well, I couldn't ask my friends or my parents, so I told him I'd be in touch if I could figure out a way. I thanked him for the rings and Coke, grabbed our drawing, and left.

I relayed all this to my buds at the beach.

Matt sympathized, "Bummer man. It sounded like he had a real plan. Guess you'll have to get a job…."

Josh was quiet, then spoke. "What if…what if we did one of those GoFundMe's? Like… other people would pledge money to see you do it."

I was suspicious. "Is that okay? Won't they prohibit it, if it's dangerous?"

"What about a porn site or underground site? This is LA. Someone's gotta have 40K to blow on some weird ass experiment." He put the word out.

Two weeks later I overheard my parents talking. Some clients mentioned a guy wanting a tunnel all the way through his body and was looking for financial supporters.

"Who'd do something that stupid?" said my dad, the guy with a rubber duck tattooed on his neck.

"Maybe they're just pushing boundaries, John. Like when I got my clit pierced," said my mom.

Really, Mom? And *Guys, it's* two *tunnels, not just one.*

Josh came through. Two weeks later he had a Russian importer, Olexei Nikitin, put up the cash and ask for an introduction. Unfortunately, it came with a big catch. They would pay for the surgery and any aftercare including additional stretching of the tunnels. But, while they were funding it, I owed them film time, during which they were allowed to do a long list of undesirable things to me using my two extra holes.

Essentially, they would be paying me a thousand dollars an hour in advance for making obscene porn movies. I told them it was a nice offer, but I wasn't interested... that shit would be on the internet forever.

Years went by, and you'd think I would have lost my desire to tunnel through. You'd also think I'd get fat. But neither happened. I started modeling, got some lucky breaks, and saved up a lot of money. But I held off on the surgery.... I didn't want to destroy my career.

One night, Nikitin's niece approached me at a party in Santa Monica, and we hit it off. I didn't know they were related since her last name was Petrov, but I found out when I went with her to her cousin's house in Malibu and Nikitin was there.

He came out of nowhere and asked me why the fuck I was at the party. I told him I was dating Nadia Petrov, and he said, "No way. You're not going near my niece, you fuckin' freak. Break it off or I'll give you a new hole through your body... through your fuckin' head," and he pulled a gun on me. I didn't want that kind of trouble, so I left without telling Nadia goodbye.

She called me up that night. "So, you really wanted to pay a surgeon to put a hole through your body?"

"They told you, huh?"

"Yes, and why would you do such a thing? You have an amazing body."

"Because no one has ever done it. And I want to show it's possible. And it's two holes by the way."

"One hole, two holes, it's all the same." A pause. "Uncle Olex says I can't date you anymore, and my mom agrees."

"What do *you* want?"

"I want a man who fights for what he believes in."

"I'm not much of a fighter compared to your family. I think I'd just end up dead."

"Putting holes through your body *is* fighting..." We sat on the phone, silent, not knowing where to take the conversation. Nadia spoke first. "Do you still want to do it?"

"Yeah, I think I do."

"Screw Uncle Olex and my mom. I'll support you. And we'll see what happens, *darling*."

At that point, I believed my modeling career was over unless it was for National Geographic. I contacted Fernando and told him to get the medical books out. We were going to make history.

In a surprisingly well-lit and sterile back room of a check cashing place in Hawthorne, Fernando inserted two 10mm surgical steel rods above my belly button and out the lumbar triangles on either side. They used what's called "regional anesthesia" on me, like when they do a C-section for babies, so I didn't feel pain in my abdomen and back, but I was awake during the whole procedure. It was a bloodbath, and I remember most of it.

I started on my back as they cut/burned through my LA with some type of hot knife / soldering iron. I could smell my flesh burning, and it made me dry-heave, but luckily I had followed Peña's orders and stopped eating well before the surgery.

The poking and prodding that ensued felt like an alien was trying to get out or into my belly. They shoved a metal device into my gut to see inside, then more and more of the device disappeared.

They flipped me on my right side and started going at it from my back. Fernando and his team spoke Spanish the whole time: I think partly to keep me in the dark about what they were doing, but, once, his assistant, said, "Oh. I *neeked* it," which sounded bad. I thought maybe they nicked my colon, but the spurts of blood all over the assistant and Fernando yelling, "*Sangre!*" at the nurse told me I was losing a lot of blood and fast... had to be a pretty big vessel. They got it under control with the soldering iron.

After what seemed like a couple of hours, they turned me over and started the second tunnel. Even reusing the front aperture and not having any major blood vessels "neeked" it still took ages. When they were done, they returned me to my right side and gave me something in an IV to put me to sleep.

The next time I woke up, someone's four-year-old kid was staring at me. He looked at me wide-eyed, like he never expected me to wake up, and then ran to the door and knocked in a pattern. A lady came to the back and told me Fernando would visit in about an hour. I'm not sure what he had that was more important, but it was south LA.... I figured someone was shot somewhere.

I couldn't see the results. I was mummified in gauze, but when Fernando arrived two hours later, he cut through it to proudly show me the rods were indeed all the way through my body. They were kept in place in the rear by a connecting silicone strap, and in the front, his ingenious "jewelry" tapered together, and the two shafts could be locked together with a small padlock.

I was on major pain meds for almost three weeks, and I had a complete lack of mobility. Fernando said the wounds would take months to stop hurting and over a year to heal. He had grafted skin in the tubes to grow around the rods. Every day, I had to unlock the locks and rotate the rods in their holes adding an anti-bacterial lubricant to aid in healing. Fortunately, nothing got infected.

Nadia and I were no longer dating, but we spoke almost every day. I told my agency I was on an indefinite leave of absence, knowing I'd never be back. After a few months, I started to regain mobility, finding new ways to work around my second pair of hip bones. My abs lost their tone, but I bought an electro-stimulus machine which worked them back into shape. Sleeping was also a bit uncomfortable, but I used an inflatable donut and a lot of pillows, which took the pressure off.

Fernando surprised me at my six-month assessment: two larger 20mm hollow tubes, inserted with a taper and threaded through my lower back. Once they were in, they felt tight and stiff again, but then he turned off the lights and shined two small flashlights through my back which came out the front with a crisscrossed beam. I totally freaked out and got emotional. It was only then that I felt like I had done it. And out of the shadow between the light beams, came Nadia. She stood on tiptoe and gave me a big kiss, saying, "You did it. You fought for what you believed in."

Over the next few years, I stretched the diameter of the tunnels to two inches in the back, leading to a single two-inch opening in the front. I now use hollow silicon inserts which give me almost the same flexibility I had before the first operation.

The feeling when I'm in the ocean, with the cool water rushing through me, is amazing. I never did any modeling again (or any porn) and only my parents and closest friends know about my body alteration. My parents were concerned about my decision to use an illicit medical facility for major surgery, but they don't mind my tunnels. My dad calls them "funnels" because he thinks using them to mix drinks would be funny.

Nadia's mom and Olex changed their minds about me when they discovered I wasn't doing this for the publicity. Oh, and I saved Olex about a half-million dollars in freight costs by hooking him up with Josh's dad, who's a customs broker. Now I work for him full-time. Nadia and I got married and we have a little boy named Andrei. I hope Andrei never gets holes or tattoos—he's perfect the way he is. But if he does, he'll have our support.

KISS MYSELF

I'm not sure when it was… the first time I met Angela. She reminded me so much of all my former girlfriends; it was like I had known her forever. But I'm getting ahead of myself.

I grew up in a big city with lots of dating options, and I really put myself out there. I guess I just got lucky that I never ended up a dad. I can't remember how many women I'd slept with. I'd occasionally think about it, or get asked by one of my buds, and thinking back, it was a lot, but it was always just one at a time.

I'd say I have a type. I like the girl next-door, who is comfortable wearing my t-shirts around the apartment and going to ball games, and drinking with the guys. I'd say that most of my girlfriends needed as much space as I did, which ultimately ended in us going our separate ways.

A few of them stick out in my mind. There was Catherine, my first girlfriend in college. She had an infectious laugh that wasn't too silly; she reminded me of Cameron Diaz in *Something About Mary*. And then there was Marta, whom I met when she delivered my Thai food. She carried a motorcycle helmet and was fearless. And then there was Michelle, who was an architect, but was onsite at her building every day getting into the nuts and bolts of the construction, not just the pretty façade. I met June, in June, and she was the first Black girl I ever dated seriously. She had a family in Delaware and was a sales rep for an auto parts company. When I looked into her eyes, I saw a reflection of myself. Come to think of it now, all these women reminded me of me in a way.

So, back to Angela....

Angela was easygoing like the rest. She gave me my space but was down for whatever came along. She worked across town at an insurance company as a claims adjuster. She had beautiful brown hair that cascaded around her perfect breasts whenever we had sex. She had the craziest sense of humor and liked to play elaborate pranks on me that took days to set up.

One Thursday, I was getting ready to go out with friends after a long work day, and I phoned Angela to see if she wanted to meet us at Jerry's on Seventh. She said she was stuck at the office but would join us later.

I met up with the guys, and *June* showed up. I hadn't seen her in years. She looked amazing, and most of my friends remembered her, so she hung out with us for a little bit to catch up. She got a call and had to leave, but as soon as she left, Marta, from way, way back walked in the place. Marta was pre-any-of-my-friends, so I introduced her. She hadn't aged a day..., hot as ever..., said she now had her own restaurant in Towson and gave me the address.

My buddy, Charles, said it was crazy that two of my exes had shown up randomly on the same day, but I shrugged it off, saying they knew Jerry's. I had brought many of my girlfriends there over the years. Marta stayed for one drink, and I was surprised she didn't run into Angela coming in through the door. Angela joined us at the bar and ordered a Coors Light. We ended up doing shots, and, at closing time, I offered to take Angela back to my place to spend the night.

We'd both had too much to drink, and we were making out on the couch in the dark like teenagers. But then something changed in Angela's breath. I opened my eyes and instead of Angela, it was a man who looked just like me. The other me laughed at me and said, "I got you good this time!" Eyes wide open, I passed out staring at myself.

I woke up the next morning, in my bed, and Angela was watching me sleep. I told her about the crazy dream I'd had where I was kissing myself. She laughed and said I might need "professional help," but then she asked me if I'd liked it.

I told her, "No. I didn't like it. It was weird."

She asked if I still had feelings for my old girlfriends. I wondered what was up, but I was honest, telling her they all had a place in my heart, but she was the only one for me. Then she asked me, "What if you could date *all* your old girlfriends at the same time, forever, and they wouldn't care?" I told her that would be awkward. And there was no chance that could *ever* happen.

And she said, "Well, what if I told you I was June, and I was Marta, and *I* was Catherine?"

I figured she knew about Marta and June from the guys at the bar the night before, but I had no idea how she knew about Catherine.

She got off the bed, did a little twirl, and she *was* Catherine. And she spun around again, and she was Marta. And again, and she was June. And once more, and she was *me*. I was in shock, but I didn't pass out. I might have said, in a baby voice, "How?"

"I'm a therian, Brian. Some people call us shapeshifters. I can change my appearance at will. I want to be with you as June or Angela or Marta or whoever, forever. I know it's a lot to process, but would you *consider* it?"

I don't know if I replied out of fear that she'd kill me with her shapeshifting powers or out of true love. Probably the former. I told her, *yes*, I'd stay with her. And to make myself feel better, I nervously joked, "As long as you don't make me kiss myself again."

"Deal!" she said, and threw her hands up in victory.

I should have been more specific. Turns out there are worse things you can kiss… than yourself.

THE ALIENS WHO SMILED BACK

Although I wasn't the first person to see the craft in the middle of the Central Park Reservoir, I knocked down two senior citizens and an occupied stroller trying to get there as fast as I could. As the host of (arguably) the top Extraterrestrial podcast in the world, *Other Earths*, I fled my Eagan, Minnesota basement with only seventy-five minutes to catch the direct to New York City.

I caught up on the news via HUD throughout the three-hour journey. Around 6:30 am, a *spaceship*, clearly not from this planet, landed in the middle of the Jacqueline Kennedy Onassis Reservoir. The reservoir used to be a primary source of water for the city, but was now only a backup, a pretty lake with a jogging track surrounding it.

Militia had cordoned off the whole north end of the park to keep civilians from gathering near the water. Officers in canoes were detaining Phelps and Ledecky wannabees vaulting the fence to swim toward the craft.

No one, not even military personnel, had approached within a hundred yards of the ship.

As my flight descended into Newark, updated images revealed the spacecraft was not floating on the water, but rather, anchored on the reservoir basin. It was shaped like a spinning top, with a bulbous body above the water tapering to a point through a columnar extension, below the surface. The unusual appendage suggested why it chose the lake instead of balancing precariously on land in the nearby park areas.

The Central Park reservoir is divided into east and west halves by a slightly-submerged wall connecting two pumphouses. The pumphouses can independently drain or fill either side of the reservoir for maintenance. The ship was positioned near the center of the wall just on the western side.

The water was heating up. As my plane took off from Minnesota, reports were that the water was at 96 degrees Fahrenheit, a forty percent increase over its nominal June temperature. When I landed in Newark (which was a madhouse, by the way), the water was already 110 and climbing. Once word got out that the world's largest hot tub was now the world's largest stew pot, no one was vaulting the fence anymore. Officials expressed concern of radiation due to the ship's unknown power source literally boiling the lake.

New Yorkers are some of the most resourceful people in the world. By the time I reached Central Park, industrious entrepreneurs had erected portable risers high enough to peek over the trees at the edge of the park and were charging admission for ten-minute views of the ship. At 88th and Central Park West, I gladly paid the $300 cash fee to a guy who looked homeless but had a wad of hundreds as thick as a brick. I ascended the rickety scaffolding toting my 40x telephoto lens. From the top I had a clear view of the circular craft 1,700 feet away.

I suppressed my desire to gaze open-mouthed at the alien craft, deciding to use my time wisely to film. I'd review my footage in minute detail later.

I got a wide shot showing the scale of the starship to be about three hundred feet in diameter and one hundred fifty feet tall above the surface of the water. As I zoomed in, I panned back and forth noting no seams in the exterior hull, like it was hewn out of a single block of dull platinum. A band of different dark material was positioned a quarter of the way from the roof. *The bridge?* And at the widest point, the sun reflected off what looked like clear glass windows, but I couldn't see anything inside.

A tap on my shoulder, and the ten minutes had passed too fast. I relinquished my spot to what sounded like a couple of young Russians and descended the precarious scaffolding. I headed back to the hotel, through the gauntlet of doomsdayers and street vendors hawking shirts already printed with accurate depictions of the spacecraft. *There's New York for ya'.*

I became worried I'd be wasting my time in the hotel. *What if the craft decided to leave... forever?* So I cut through, to the Park's east side, searching for anywhere to breach security. I found it in the form of a press director granting access to the roof of the Guggenheim. As a legitimate journalist, I held a press pass, although it took some coaxing to compete for one of the limited spots.

This was *way* better than the scaffolding... free admission *and* an unobstructed view of the craft on a stable building. I was also three hundred feet closer. However, higher was not necessarily better. I couldn't see the bank of clear windows I'd spotted before. But we had access to regular briefings from Judith Cann, the Deputy Director of Homeland Security, and high-quality photos and drone video footage before it ever broke to the public.

I appropriated a triangular corner of the roof with a line of sight to the spacecraft on one side and the roof egress from the museum on the other. I could monitor any ship activity and the ongoings of other reporters as they went in and out of the building.

I posted a video for the *Other Earths* fanbase live from the Guggenheim, and it was a hit. I was careful not to leak anything that wasn't public knowledge. I didn't want to jeopardize my access at the rooftop.

A mist, then a fog, started to envelop the ship. Word spread among the press community that the water was boiling.

At 7:30 pm there were a couple of video announcements and a breakthrough.

First of all, they confirmed the temperature of the reservoir had briefly reached its boiling point, and through evaporation the water level had dropped ten feet, exposing the wall connecting the pumphouses. The water temperature was currently at 180 degrees and dropping. One protestor had achieved suicide by jumping the fence and blistering to death.

Secondly, as of then, we were unable to identify how many life forms might be aboard. Infra-red imaging would not penetrate the hull, and the clear windows must not be glass.

The most significant breakthrough was the sighting of two small humanoids appearing in the glass-like enclosure. They looked out over the park, with broad smiles on their faces as they pointed across the lake. They also appeared to be pointing at various buildings. They were in the window for about two minutes, and then disappeared.

The footage of the aliens was a little distorted, but it did appear to be a couple of happy children playing at the window. Their heads were slightly larger than ours and dominated by a huge smiling mouth. *Like the old ad for Sea Monkeys where the King and Queen and children Sea Monkeys were always smiling. Big smiles, big eyes, high cheekbones, and frail bodies.* They appeared to be clothed, which was surprising. I always suspected aliens would be naked. Their skin was blueish-gray, not green. *Another stereotype down the drain.*

Judith Cann completed her update with a statement about contact. The military tried to message the visitors through the whole gamut of radio frequencies, but had not yet established communication. Nor had we detected any messaging from them. Either our signals were unable to penetrate the hull, or its residents did not feel like responding. Also, whenever our camera drones would fly too close, their electronics would fail, like they were being jammed. Our guests wanted to keep their privacy, so far.

Judith signed off from her control center and the rooftop lit up with live updates and bootleg pictures of the kids smiling from the spacecraft.

Since no one knew the sex of the beings, NBC named them Chris and Pat based an old recurring *Saturday Night Live* skit, "It's Pat!," in which the androgynous main character's sex is never revealed.

After my 8 p.m. update and other "reaction" posts through my normal channels, I noticed that I was not the only podcaster who'd made it through the credential gauntlet. Miranda Evers from *Night Eye* was also there. We had a friendly rivalry for subscribers, with about seventy percent of the total English-speaking market, and about half of our subscribers shared. Those who thirsted for alien truths were not likely to align with only one source.

Miranda is a hot lesbian I had tried to convert more than once. Sometimes she lets me feel like I might be making progress, but deep down I know she's just fucking with me. I'm okay with that too.

When we spotted each other we agreed to collab, taking shifts sleeping and monitoring to stay current yet manage our energy. I trust Miranda, so I let her take the first shift and got a little shut-eye. I'm surprised I could sleep with such craziness going on, but I was more tired than I thought. She woke me at 11:30 pm saying the ship was making noises.

I must've been dead to the world, to not wake up and hear that hideous sound. *An asthmatic goose mimicking a slide whistle.* A bizarre up and down pitch with a vibrato in it and not on any musical scale I'd ever heard. I thought, *So now we know aliens are tone deaf.* The dissonance continued for four hours. It never varied, as far as I could tell. Just up… and down. Up… down. It was like they were trying to get us to go away. I put on my headphones and listened to the hardest rock I could stand to block out the cacophony.

When the sound finally stopped, Judith Cann confirmed we had not yet been able to decipher the message from the aliens. Probably because there was none. Other than four hours of Fuck…off. Fuck…off. She divulged that the signal appeared to come, not from speakers, but from the whole ship resonating.

I let Miranda sleep until the sun shone through the buildings east of the museum, illuminating the west reservoir and the gunmetal gray ship. The black windows were now facing us directly. The ship had turned ninety degrees counterclockwise to face us. We still couldn't see the clear windows well, but the rooftop monitors relayed coverage from the track.

Chris and Pat showed up at their window at 9:30 am. It looked like they were smiling and waving to the crowd, but I think that was our overactive imaginations, reading something into the side-to-side movements of their frail arms.

I was hoping we would have a better game plan for reaching them on day two. The sky that morning was full of unsanctioned drones. None of them got any closer than the official ones. and most fell into the scalding reservoir, which, per reports, had stabilized at *only* 140 degrees.

The military intelligence teams erected a Times-Square-sized TV screen on the track running alongside Central Park East, directed at the ship. On it they began to show videos and images of Earthly activities and simple words in various languages. According to Carr, their aim was to educate and urge the visitors to reciprocate. But as of now, besides Chris and Pat, we had no contact at all.

Miranda and I gazed out at the ship all day. We laughed about how our mutual life obsession had come true, did a collab podcast, and even toasted the aliens with champagne provided to the press by the museum. By the end of the day we still couldn't tell if they were just refueling, broken down, or here for some other reason. Until nightfall.

Around 8:45 p.m. on the second night, after sundown, the ship illuminated a single spot on its surface, between the two bays of windows: like their own movie screen thirty feet high and sixty feet across. The positioning of it was perfect for Miranda and me.

The aliens started displaying images like the ones from our video screen, and I realized they were telling a story. They didn't *need* words to communicate with us. They showed a spaceship like theirs making stops at various planets across the universe. They were gathering specimens, like an outer-space Noah's Ark: animals and other human-like creatures. We couldn't tell from the movie if it was just a plan, and we were the first stop, or if they had a host of intergalactic creatures aboard. The ten-minute show looped five times and went dark.

And the shopping list began...

Clear video of a harbor seal from the Central Park Zoo. *Wow. It had to be a mile and a half away.*

A dog yapping in the window of an apartment on Central Park West.

Miranda and me, toasting champagne to the ship.

Miranda gasped as our images projected on the screen. *Did they really mean us? Or just two humans?*

The nearby reporters were murmuring, and I sensed their bright camera lights shining on us from the side.

I think we were both in shock. Surely, they had just taken a picture of something they saw... a representative life form, not specifically us. I said as much to Miranda.

But Miranda put her arms in a V to signal the visitors that she was willing to be the actual volunteer. I just went with it. I grabbed her hand in my own V, and they broadcast us on the ship screen, confirming it really *was* us they were watching.

At the time, caught up in the moment of celebrity, knowing our podcasts were going viral, and we were the hottest celebrities in the world, I didn't stop to think about our lives ending. But as the military arrived to take us to the ship I started to panic. Miranda told me we'd be okay. That the smiling aliens did not wish us any harm. They were researchers and would want to study us. We'd be in a high-tech zoo, and they'd take care of us.

I wasn't so sure. *How would they be able to sustain our need for oxygen and food?* Best case was we'd end up in some type of cryochamber or suspended in liquid in a "Hall of Beings" for the amusement of Chris and Pat and their little birthday party friends. Worst case would be dissection. No… *live* dissection.

But Miranda said we had this "one chance" to gain insight into our vocation. It was worth the risk. Worst case for her was being rejected and not allowed to board the ship.

We were taken to the base headquarters at the Central Park NYPD near the south gatehouse. The video instructions were clear. The animals and humans were to be placed on the retaining wall near the ship at the center of the reservoir.

We were being outfitted with safety and tactical and recording gear when we heard a commotion. The ship was moving. I donned my HUD in time to watch the live footage of the full craft ascending out of the water and onto the reservoir wall, balancing on its tip, which couldn't have been more than five feet across. It *did* resemble a giant top. They must have had some incredible gyroscopes because it was rock solid, not wobbling at all, like it had been built there. It was even more majestic than I expected. Miranda was also watching on her HUD with her mouth open. And she *may* have let out a *"Fuck yeah."*

The harbor seal and a dog, which to me didn't look like "The Dog," were crated and prepped at the gatehouse. Two military personnel rowed them to the center of the lake and placed them on the wall. Chris and Pat appeared at the window with a third child who peeked out for only a moment, then retreated out of view. I'm sure new names were flying across the internet within ten seconds.

The officer in charge let us know that the dog and seal were a test. If they were accepted, we would assume the aliens didn't specifically need Miranda and me to board the ship. They would send two trained operatives in our place.

A secondary column descended from below the bank of clear windows and the seal and dog were retrieved from the wall, like one of those vacuum suction tubes from the bank. The column went up into the ship and back down.

Dead seal, dead dog, back on the wall. Video showing requested seal. Video showing requested dog. Video showing Miranda and me.

Chris and Pat were still smiling as the dead animals were retrieved. Maybe the smile wasn't genuine. Maybe a sea monkey can *only* smile. Or maybe they thought they were playing a game.

It was crystal clear that we were the subjects. But when we appeared at the gatehouse covered in tactical gear the goosey slide whistle sound started, and the movie came on. And a naked man and woman showed on the screen. *Oh boy.* They weren't going to let us take anything aboard.

Miranda was already stripping, against the advice of the commander. I followed suit. Chris and Pat were pointing and smiling, and though I felt like was going to shit myself, we descended to the rocky wall and started to walk toward the ship. My legs didn't want to go with us. My heart was beating so hard I could hear it, wondering if we were going to be accepted or discarded like trash because we didn't meet the criteria. The real dog and seal were being delivered ahead of us. We would get a preview.

The column came down and took the two animals up to the ship. This time when the column returned it was empty. *Acceptance.* I expected Chris and Pat to be holding the dog in the window, but they were still just there watching us and waving their freakin' thin arms around, slowly, as if they were on a float during the Macy's Thanksgiving Day parade.

I imagined how my life might change forever with Miranda and me being surrogate parents to Chris and Pat: a stupid fantasy that framed the uncertainty into a more pleasant outcome and allowed me to complete the distance to the center of the wall.

When we arrived, a circular light beam illuminated the spot on the wall where we were to stand. *That's how the military knew where to place the animals.* We stepped onto the circle and the column came down to retrieve us.

As the tunnel surrounded us, everything went completely dark, and I believe we were anesthetized because I don't remember anything until I woke up lying on a cushion of air, just above the floor, with Pat and Chris staring down at me. I had on an oxygen helmet, and I could move my eyes, but otherwise, I was paralyzed. Then I was "floated up?" to the kids' level and Pat (or maybe Chris) took my hand, and I saw a movie in my head of who they were and why they were here.

Chris and Pat were not children. Along with a crew of three, they were adult aliens who had lived for possibly hundreds of years traveling with the hope of finding other intelligent life. And though they thought many things I could not grasp, I got the gist of their feelings about us: pleased they had found life, but disappointed we were not as evolved as they were. All the while smiling those stupid smiles which I now knew were genetically painted on their faces.

They sensed our fear and uncertainty and gave us a snack through the helmet. A treat, like we would give a dog. I wanted to know, were we still in Central Park? Were we millions of miles out into deep space? What was our future?

Chris (or maybe Pat) took my hand once more. And I saw my future. An operation to help me breathe the ship's atmosphere, a long life of traveling and learning, and a strange new family, with a seal and a dog as pets, and five alien parents who'd made our dreams come true.

CLUB CEMETERY

Although we lived several hundred miles apart, my old high school friend, Artie, and I would alternate visits every couple of years. He'd drive down to visit me in Norfolk, or I'd head up to Long Island for a week. We'd take off work and go fishing and play golf.

Our wives would find something to do out of town so they wouldn't have to put up with our bullshit, which was really just some late-night drinking and loudness... harmless guy-fun. But two years ago, we experienced some *weird shit* that changed both of us forever. I now believe in the afterlife because I've seen ghosts, and I've seen them party.

Artie lives in Stony Brook, on the north side of the Island, not far from the Sound. We grew up in nearby Farmingdale, but I moved away after high school to go to Old Dominion.

I love Virginia, but I miss my hometown, and seeing Artie. We used to have so much fun hanging out and listening to Blue Öyster Cult, who are also from Stony Brook. I kid Artie that he moved there and took a job at Stony Brook University because he couldn't get a gig as a BÖC roadie. But really he and his wife, Cynthia, still have a lot of family nearby. My dad died when I was in college, and my mom passed away about ten years later, so I had no one left in the area except for Artie.

Artie was a member at Colonial Springs Golf Club in Farmingdale. On Tuesday we took a late tee time and played the Lakes/Pines track, which, coincidentally, backs up to the Beth Moses Cemetery where my folks are buried.

We finished the last hole at almost dark, then headed to the nearby Taco Bell. I still had a bunch of tees in my pocket, and I had Artie pop the trunk, so I could throw them in my bag, and damn if my leather Ferrari three-wood headcover was gone.

I remembered right away where it was. Artie and I were coming off the par five, fourth hole, and we got into a headcover fight. I was imitating him using his *Caddyshack* gopher headcover as a ventriloquist doll and took it with me when I went to take a piss in the pines. I acted like his Gopher was giving head. In retribution, he grabbed my $150 Ferrari cover and pretended to wipe his ass with it. Then he threw it into the woods. I'd meant to go pick it up, but I forgot.

When I indicated we should snag it on the way home, Artie said, "Forget it - I'll buy you another one." But when I told him how much it cost, he changed his mind.

First, we stopped and got some beer for our "adventure," then tried to park at the cemetery, right next to the hole, but all the gates were closed. So we parked at the club and headed out across the course. Just our luck, the fourth tee box is about the farthest point from the clubhouse, but we had decent moonlight and a six-pack of Brooklyn Lager, my favorite.

When we got to four, I went toward the woods and found the headcover right away. Since we were already there, I told Artie we should visit my parents' graves. I knew they were in the part of the cemetery close to the golf course.

Artie was game, so we scrambled through the trees and bushes separating the golf course from the cemetery. I tried to get my bearings. We were near a corner sign for North Street and Maccabee. I remembered my parents being off South Street, so we walked south down Maccabee, hoping to hit it.

In the distance, a mass of smoke or steam was rising from the street near the next intersection. *Maybe a water main break? Or a sprinkler malfunction?*.

As we got closer, it resembled one of those fog machines you'd see at a dance club or when the players emerge from a tunnel at a football game. But inside the fog, it looked like human shapes writhing about. I asked Artie if he could make out human-like shapes in it, and he just nodded with his mouth open staring at them. I got out my phone and started filming, but it was too grainy in the low light.

I suggested we get closer, but Artie declined, saying, "Nah, I'm good. It's spooky... looks like ghosts... dancing."

I completely agreed, but for whatever reason, I was not fearful of it, just fascinated. Many ghostlike figures in various states of human and gaseous form, overlapping. And it seemed like they were pulsing, in sync, like they were boogying to inaudible music.

Artie took several steps back, but I was drawn in. Closer and closer, slowly, as if they noticed me they would instantly vanish. I was only about ten feet away when, in the fog, my mother's face appeared, almost like it was pressed up against a glass boundary between us. I cried out "Mom!" and suddenly all movement stopped, the vapor dissipated, and I was standing alone at Maccabee and South.

Artie had seen what I saw... my mom in the foggy cloud. There was no explanation for how we both experienced the same thing except that it had existed. I told him, "I don't think we need to find the graves anymore."

As we walked back across the course, we were in shock that we had witnessed the afterlife, but I also felt a curious joy. There were good vibes, and my mom was having a blast.

I've gone back, several times after dark, and I now know my parents' graves are only a block away from where we saw the fog, but I've never seen that phenomenon again. And I learned one other strange and coincidental fact:

One of the people buried near Maccabee and South was entrepreneur Steve Rubell, a founder of the infamous Studio 54 disco in New York City. Steve died twenty years *to the day* that we had been in that cemetery. Apparently, Steve's got a *new* club, and my mom likes to dance there whenever it's open.

HEAVEN'S ON THE OTHER SIDE OF A CHAIN LINK FENCE

I moved to a mid-sized town in Texas a few years ago. My property backed up to an old stone quarry site recently purchased by the city. The developers had plans to fill it and use it as a water supply and recreational area. The new homesites on my side were extra-wide lots with large backyards set to look out over the new lake. It promised to be a fantastic view once they finished the project.

When I moved in, though, my view was of an eight-foot tall chain link fence that wrapped completely around the quarry to protect the city from liability. That made sense, but it sure was an eyesore.

My Yorkie, Buster, and I circled the quarry for exercise most every day. There was a twenty-foot easement between the city property and the ranch-style back fences of the residents. The plan was to make it a formal hike-and-bike trail after the lake was finished, but then it was just uneven dirt and trodden grass from the casual jogger.

Buster and the other dogs would play "trump your dump" trying to mark their territory. He had his favorite spots to stop, but there was one particular spot at the right edge of my lot, where the Altstadt's property started. Buster'd drop down on his front haunches, put his snout through the two-inch aperture, and jump back barking, then do it again, over and over until I made him leave. Sometimes he'd whine and then bark. I'd check for birds or other animals but never saw a thing.

He made such a ruckus, the Altstadt's and their lab Frida would leave their back porch and go inside. I never thought of them as friendly people. They called the homeowner association because I left my unpainted Chevy Camaro in the driveway too long. I moved their trash can three houses down in retribution. We've hardly spoken a word since.

One evening at dusk, Buster and I went out for a short walk slightly past the Altstadt's property and back, no more than a quarter-mile. Buster darted to his spot, and I bent to tie my shoe about two feet from him. As he started his ritual, I knew he had to be seeing something. He'd look through the fence, stick his nose in it, then jump back and bark. Since I was already down at his level, I lay down on the ground and looked through the hole. And I saw something. Not the grass growing up on the thin edge of the quarry cliff. Not people walking around the other side of the quarry or the opposing rock wall. I saw Heaven.

I hadn't drunk any alcohol; I don't do drugs, but my logical mind and my eyes were not getting along. Through the opening I saw a short, hazy tunnel the color of the weeds and grasses on the other side of the fence. Looking through the hole at any angle other than directly straight, it would appear normal. But beyond the dusk-colored three-inch-long rhomboid tunnel was the bluest sky I'd ever seen and the fluffiest clouds with just the right amount of light hitting them. I was entranced. I didn't see any people, only sky and clouds, but it was fascinating and peaceful, and I was filled with a hope of something I didn't understand, but might someday.

I returned to the house to get my camera to film it. Buster went willingly. I guess he'd seen Heaven hundreds of times and knew it'd be there when we got back.

It was.

I held the camera to the opening and recorded a video. I watched it on the screen, but it was unextraordinary, like a fuzzy screensaver. But perhaps it was proof. I didn't know if I had captured Heaven or a portal to another dimension, but given how little I knew of either, it didn't matter. I had always thought of Heaven as a step up from a parallel dimension, and what I saw through the fence sure seemed like an improvement over Earth.

I went home and passed out from exhaustion and my mind going crazy. The next morning I went out at dawn to peer through the hole again. This time, my grandma was sitting at a kitchen table smiling at an unknown person, maybe Grandpa. She was happy, and I was happy for her. She gazed forward enthralled with her companion, her mouth slightly parted, anticipating every word the person across from her had to say.

Seeing Grandma solidified that it was indeed Heaven and not just another dimension. *Where else would Grandma be?*

I gave Buster a turn to sniff and bark at Grandma or cats or whatever he saw on the other side.

I looked back into the hole one more time. Only blue sky and fluffy clouds that time, but I wasn't sad. I was content with what I was watching.

On the third day when I looked I saw my mother baking a pie, and saw her set it on the countertop to cool. The light from somewhere shone on her face, and she was beautiful, not harrowed and blotchy from the cancer that had taken her four years ago. Being with her again, I felt relieved and welcomed. I shouted out to her, but she went on about her business. I wasn't disappointed. It seemed I was capable of only positive feelings when looking through the fence, like, *maybe I'm in Heaven, too.*

My mother looked around for a while as if she had forever, so I left. *That's what we do on Earth. When we feel like our time is up, we leave. But in Heaven, maybe an hour is a year, and we stay.*

I was selfish. I kept the secret to myself for eight days. But on the ninth day, as I was looking through the fence, Hank Altstadt scared the shit out of me.

"What the Hell you doin' down there on the ground?" he asked sharply.

I don't think Hank and I had said two words to each other in the five months since we'd been neighbors. I was trying to make up a lie when he said, "I seen you down there five times now. You and your yappin' dog."

I decided to break the ice. "Look through this hole and tell me what you see."

He got down on the ground and looked through the fence and said, "What the Hell?" He had seen Heaven.

He was mumbling, so I couldn't understand, but as Hank pulled away after twenty minutes he shook his head. His best friend, who had died in Vietnam, was playing with his daughter on a tire swing. He had a jagged scar down his right cheek, but he acted stronger, more self-assured than the kid Hank'd known in '71.

Hank and I agreed to tell his wife, Marjorie, but no one else. "Guess that dog was onto something. We thought he was just *on* something."

\#

Marjorie bent her head down to the ground. She couldn't see anything. We moved her to the correct hole, and she said, "Oh my! It's beautiful!" I asked if there were clouds and blue sky, and she said no, it was a waterfall, with naked girls in it. Hank and I glanced at each other, wondering why we didn't get naked girls, but that's what she got.

And when Marjorie got up she was all aglow, like she had been reborn.

Witnessing Heaven through a chain link fence isn't one thing over and over. It's a bunch of things that all make you happy in a variety of ways. Once I saw neon lights that reminded me of my childhood in the 80's. Like a fantastic dream I couldn't control, it always ended up being something I liked. No, not liked... *loved.*

One afternoon, as we were taking turns peering through the fence and looking out for joggers, we noticed they were filling in the quarry. It felt like it hadn't even been a month since we found the hole, but in reality, it had been six. We had lost half a year peering through the fence, daily, often for hours at a time.

Knowing they would remove the fence after the quarry was full, we carefully clipped out a square foot of the fence surrounding the hole. We expected the portal to be lost forever, and when Hank looked through the hole all he saw was me. But I saw clouds running through his head.

"It's backward, Hank," I said, thinking, *we did it. We saved the view of Heaven.* Buster was about to jump through the new hole in the real fence, and I had to snatch him before he did. We cut another piece of fence farther up and used it to cover the piece we'd cut out. I peered through the replacement fence, right where the old hole was. Just quarry.

Maybe there are other holes in other chain link fences with views of Heaven. Sometimes, when I'm walking by one, I'll check what's on the other side, but so far, what Buster and Hank and Marjorie and I had seen was special.

The new lake is a beautiful addition to our backyards, but I've seen better. I *do* see better, every day. The cutout fence is mounted between our properties, using a swivel so that it can be rotated either way. I generally use it at night, and the Altstadts use it during the day. And we never fight about it because we know what awaits us if we are virtuous.

MARY NICHOLS HIGHWAY

I was on hour fourteen, driving the last bit of Highway 71 into Austin from the west. My plan was to cut at least one hour off the sixteen-hour drive from Laramie to reach my buddy's house by 8 p.m., but the trip was more taxing than I anticipated.

I had done a couple long road trips before (everything's far from Laramie), and it was not unusual for me to have to push past the barriers. In my teens and early twenties, I'd hit up a truck stop for some "Trucker speed" called Mini-thins, which were basically ephedrine, and I could drive all night. But this time I'd settled for a double shot Starbucks in Lubbock, which worked until the brutal stretch I was on. And when I get overtired, I start hallucinating.

I remember driving from Denver back to Laramie, after a night out on the town. I could have sworn that a peloton of cyclists was in the lane right next to me. Not even ghostly or blurry. I knew it wasn't real, and I was hallucinating, so I ended up pulling over and sleeping it off.

This time, when I started seeing hundreds and thousands of small white crosses on the side of the road, I thought *Here we go again.*

Like a Potter's field, the crosses went on for a mile, then two. I pulled over thinking I was having a stroke. *There's no way this many people died on a perfectly straight stretch of highway.*

I put on my hazard lights, and checking for the high-speed traffic behind me, I got out to a sea of very real crosses. Forty of them within a few feet of my car. Each one had a name and date. I remember the first one I saw was Meredith Meadows, and the dates indicated she was a three-year-old child.

I went to the next and the next and they all indicated the victims were between two and seven years old.

The crosses were simple white boards with four long nails holding them together. The writing was black paint, but meticulously done, almost calligraphy. One of the weirdest things was that the dates for a group of crosses were not the same. If a car or bus of children had wrecked here, they'd all be the same date. *And why would so many two-year-olds be on the same bus?* It didn't add up.

My curiosity was resolved when the trees rustled and a pair of deer eyes stared at me from the cover, fifty feet from the traffic. I knew immediately I was looking at crosses for dead deer.

At this point, I was awake. I phoned my buddy, and said I'd be a little late, got back in my car, and continued down the road to a roadside restaurant named Angie's. I figured I could rest, refuel, and get the scoop on the insane cross-building culture of this area.

Angie's was a no-nonsense diner, featuring burgers, and chicken fried steak, and cold beer. Country music was playing on the speakers, and the place was empty except for a couple of patrons at the bar. The bartender waved her hand at the four tables and said, "Sit anywhere, Sugar."

I sat at the farthest table from the bar, and when she came to ask me," Watcha drinkin', Sugar?" I popped the question.

"What's with all the crosses? Are they for deer?"

"Oh, honey, you're not from around here are ya?"

"Nope, Laramie, Wyoming. I was passing through after driving all day, and I thought I was seeing things—"

"You drove all the way from Wyoming today? Honey, you need to rest. And you came to the right place. We got the best chicken-fried out here, and 'ol Bill…," she motioned to a guy in a plaid shirt and cowboy hat, "he'll get you up to speed real quick on them crosses. What's your name, hon?"

"Jeff Hayes."

"Bill, baby, we got us another visitor. He's from Wyoming and drove all day. You mind tellin' him 'bout Mary's crosses?"

"Well, no problem, Miss Angie." Then to me, "Come join us at the bar, young fella. I'll get you all caught up real good on them crosses."

I joined Bill and his friends, Clive and Marty, at the bar. Clive and Marty resumed talking about the upcoming Texas football game, and Bill turned his attention to me. Though he'd told the story hundreds of times, he didn't act the least bit irritated that he was asked to tell it again.

Angie brought me an ice-cold Shiner Bock, and though it was against my better judgment, I accepted. *Just one beer*….

I started the conversation with, "Are those crosses all for deer?"

"Yup. You sure you never heard of Mary Nichols Highway? That was a pretty good guess, and almost right."

I told him how I'd seen the deer staring at me while I was checking out the crosses.

He nodded and said, "Lemme start you at the beginnin', cause it's more interestin' that way. We got a lot of deer down in these parts. And you can't hunt 'em unless it's deer season, so they get real populous. We got a bunch of creeks from the Colorado River and lots of brush, so they multiply like rabbits out here. But they ain't so smart. Now I bet you was doin' seventy or eighty down the highway."

"Ninety. Trying to make good time."

"Oh, yeah, Wyomin' 'n one day. Impressive. Well, them deer just jump out like they have a death wish, or they wanna control their own population. I don't know how they avoid cars as babies, but come about two or three years old they think they can make it across the highway. And they don't."

"Like Frogger," I volunteered.

"Um, I don't know what that is, but, yeah. We see them deer every day on the side of the road. Clive here's brother bought a thousand acres off of towing people's wrecked cars.

"So, there was this woman named Mary Nichols. She didn't live here; she lived in Round Mountain, which is 'round the way, off 281. Well, Mary wasn't from around here originally. She was from New York and only came here 'cause her sister was dying of leukemia or something. And one day she saw a dead deer on the side of the road, and she was real beat up about it. She stopped at the Spicewood store and got a couple of pieces of wood and a shovel, and she buried that deer right there on the spot and put up a cross.

"Now, we all thought that a peculiar thing to do, but it was kinda a nice gesture. We just knew it wouldn't last long. If she wanted to keep that up, she'd be runnin' outta wood. And dirt. Out here, the Department of Transportation removes the animals from the highway after two or three days, so we don't pay it no mind. Just a part of life.

"Well, Miss Mary didn't give up so easy. She found another deer, and another. And she figgered she couldn't bury 'em all, so she'd call 'em in, and then put up a cross. And she gave every one of them a deer name and a date of birth. She got real good at estimatin' how old they were by lookin' at their teeth and bellies."

Angie plopped down a massive chicken fried steak with cream gravy and fries. And another Shiner. I remember thinking, *Imma be here a while.*

Bill encouraged me to eat. "Ooooh. Them steaks are real good. You might be driving down from Wyomin' once a week after you get a taste of that one."

I cut off a piece and popped it in my mouth. It melted, and I thought, *I could eat one of these every day for the rest of my life.* I joked, "Deer meat?"

Bill laughed. "Nope, good ol' cow, but if you've got a taste for venison, I could get you some." He finished his beer, and Angie had another already waiting to swap out. He continued with the story.

"So, that first year, I reckon Mary put up two hundred crosses. She was on 71 most every day, walking from Miller's Point to the farmhouse about two miles back where you see them crosses end. That was the Green's place, and they didn't want no crosses blocking their property. So Mary stopped there. It drove her crazy when a deer would die past that spot, but she had enough to do with just her three miles. She'd call it in to TxDot for pick-up, but respected the Green's wishes and didn't put up no crosses there.

"I think this is why she started doin' the other side too. So then she had six miles. It was about this time that her sister Lois—"

"Lou-ise," Angie corrected him, and to me, "He's knows it's Louise; he just likes to mess with me."

Bill tapped his temple, "Oh yeah, you're right… Lou-eeeeese. Well, Louise died.

"And we didn't know she died, but we figgered it out when the number of crosses started going up. Seemed Mary had a lot more free time for her hobby now that she didn't have to take care of her sister. We thought maybe she'd move back to New York, but she didn't.

"After a couple more years, she started calling in skunks and possums and armadillos. And they'd get small, little crosses you won't even see sticking up above the weeds. I think she found an endless supply of wood and at night she'd go make crosses and then ever' mornin' park her car off Miller's road and load up her wagon, walk the three miles up one side then down the other. Ever' day. In five years, the paper said she had put up thirty-five hundred crosses.

"Then, one day, she was pullin' her cart over on the north side about halfway through her route and a car blew a tire, skidded sideways and took her out. *Irony* is what I call that. The hospital chopper arrived in fifteen minutes, but she was dead on site. We considered calling TxDot to have her removed, because that's what she would have wanted."

Angie shook her head, "Not true."

"The people around here said she should be buried right there, but the state wouldn't allow it, so they buried her near her sister. But we all put up a big cross on that spot and got one of them official signs that says, "Mary Nichols Highway.""

I replied, "Bummer. RIP Mary. Thanks for getting me caught up."

"Oh, that ain't it."

Two more Shiners appeared out of nowhere.

"Uh oh. Then what?"

"People like you'self started gettin' into wrecks around here. They were swervin' off the road claiming to see a woman walking across the highway with a cart. None of us here ever seen it, but Danny's wife said she saw sump'n in the road one day, and she swears it was Mary's ghost."

"You'd think there'd be a bunch of ghost deer too."

"Oh, no. If you see a Mary ghost, you can drive right through, but them deer are real."

Noted.

"But here's the weirdest part…" Bill leaned in real close and shook his head from side to side. "We ain't had a dead deer on that stretch since she died. It's like her ghost is keepin' them deer off the road."

I thanked Bill for telling me the story and finished my beer. I had renewed energy, and the guys said I should be okay to drive now that we were well past sundown: the deer would be sleeping.

I had a great week in Austin, but the highlight of my trip was seeing the crosses and hearing the story of Mary Nichols. On the way back to Wyoming, I took a few extra minutes to pull off the road to visit Mary's cross. It was early morning, and in the hazy dawn, deer eyes monitored me from the safety of the thicket, making sure my intentions at her memorial were noble.

THE HEDGE

I was eight when we gave Grandma to the hedge. That was my first time to experience death and the effect it had on the living. My mom was a basket case. Grandma had lived with us for the previous five years, and even though she had been in the hospital for three weeks, Mom kept reassuring us she would get better and come home soon.

Things moved quickly. I was called into the principal's office during recess. They told me Grandma had died.

"And?" I asked.

"And your dad will be here to pick you up in a few minutes to take her to the Hedge."

I knew about the Hedge. School bullies would threaten the smaller kids saying they'd take them to the Hedge if they didn't give up their pudding, but most of them didn't have first-hand knowledge of it. One kid, Dicky, had to give his mom to the Hedge when we were in kindergarten, but he told me he didn't really understand what was going on.

Dad picked me up, and Kaylee was in the car already. She only went to school half-days because she had special needs. She didn't know what we were doing, and I think that was good, because sometimes she could get set off by minor things.

Since Grandma lived with us, we were all expected to go, but I didn't know if I wanted to. Of course, I was a little curious what the Hedge was all about, but I was also a little scared. Dad sensed this and told me the Hedge would make sure we didn't get sick. He said that, in the old times, people would be buried in the ground and diseases would get spread, but the Hedge took care of that problem, killing the diseases and turning the people into clean air for us to breathe. I thought about breathing in Grandma. She had a distinct and unpleasant odor. He wasn't exactly making things better.

Dad also said that if I didn't want to watch I didn't have to. He said sometimes people get upset and that Mom will probably be very sad, but Kaylee and I just needed to give her our hugs and emotional support.

Outside of town, we drove across a flat field that looked like it went on forever. On either side of us, where I had expected crops to be grown, were only wild grasses. Dad said this was called "the Barrier" and it was a good way to separate the town from the Hedge. He said both sides of the Hedge had such a barrier, but in some areas of the country there was not enough land, and the hedge was protected by high walls.

As we neared the Hedge I was surprised by how tall it was. We parked by Mom's car and there was also a hearse and the Mayor's car, which I recognized from the little flags on the front. We were all about a hundred yards from the Hedge.

I guess I expected the Hedge to be manicured, but it was unruly. Some of the branches and leaves were sticking out of the sides and the top. It made sense that people shouldn't go near it just to trim it.

Looking to the left and the right it looked like the Hedge went on forever. I asked Dad how people got to the other side of the Hedge and if it was all one big hedge across the country. He said people built bridges over it, too high for the Hedge to reach. He said there was one in Johnson City, which I remembered because we went to the fair there, and I rode a black and white pony, and I'd named it Johnson.

Grandma lay on a stretcher, and Mom was by her. Grandma had a sheet covering her whole body but not her face. Kaylee and I stayed away. I didn't want to be near a dead person.

Dad went over and spoke with the Mayor and a tall man who I learned was the undertaker. The undertaker was in a brown suit, which was maybe a little small for him, and I thought he probably had a hard time finding clothes because he was so tall... at least a foot taller than Dad and for sure the tallest guy I had ever seen. He also had a rope hanging off to the side, which made him look like a cowboy.

The priest pulled up in a black car. Dad told me Grandma was already in heaven, so the priest was not there for her, but for us. He walked over to my mom and said a prayer for her and touched her forehead, and then he gave her a hug.

The Mayor checked his pocket watch and said it was time.

The undertaker bowed to Mom and Dad, and they stepped away from the stretcher. He pushed Grandma toward the Hedge and the stretcher bounced all over the uneven ground. For a second I thought it would be funny if Grandma bounced off the stretcher and fell off onto the grass, but then I corrected myself. I was supposed to be serious.

Kaylee was preoccupied with some rocks and a stick, so I left her and joined Mom and Dad who were a little closer to the Hedge. I gave Mom a hug around her butt.

When the undertaker was about thirty feet in front of the Hedge, he tied the rope around his waist, looped it through the handle of the stretcher, and tied it to a six-foot tall pole sticking out of the ground.

He then removed the sheet from Grandma, and I could see she was naked, which was gross. And she was not on a mattress, just the bare metal stretcher. The undertaker pushed her toward the hedge, and we couldn't see her very well in front of him.

When he reached the Hedge, the rope was tight between him and the pole. He wasn't going to be able to go any further. He raised the closest edge of the stretcher about seven feet off the ground. She slid down the slick metal ramp headfirst until the hedge stopped her.

This was only temporary. Grandma's head was drawn into the hedge, and, slowly, so was the rest of her. Mom was crying and I was hugging her. And I felt different. Like Grandma was dead before, but now she was also *gone*. I started to cry too.

Dad said she is part of the Hedge, and she will always be there. And when I thought about it that way, I realized she wasn't gone any more than she was before. So, on the way back to the car, I skipped ahead of Kaylee and enjoyed the new, clean air she made.

SOUL-LETTING

Soul-letting, or soul-transference, is the practice of creating purposeful apertures in the living human body for one or more souls to leave or enter to rebalance the Id, Ego, and Superego. Souls are neither good nor bad, just compatible or incompatible, and incompatible souls from one host will eventually take up residence in, and heal, another.

The basis for this rite is an unspoken knowledge, which has taken more popular variations in bloodletting, trepanning, and exorcism. The desounen ritual of Haitian Vodou has elements of these beliefs, albeit on the non-living body. But it is in the farthest corners of the world where this ceremony is still performed in its purest and most effective form, as it has been for centuries.

Candidates are brought forward from family members, tribal leaders, and in some cases self-admittance, and selected based on the evaluation of the tribe physician. The physician, trained by a former tribal doctor, evaluates through objective and subjective means, using signs, some of which are evident only to him or her. Belief is an important aspect of the service. The treatment is not optional. Once a candidate is chosen completing the ritual is in the best interest of the host and the family.

Each tribe uses its own protocols for song, dress, and other preparations, but the heart of the procedure is standard. The host body is cleaned and stripped of all garments and a sharp instrument is used to make precise cuts at hundreds of places on the body, portals for the souls to enter and exit. The balance of the souls is vital as the host cannot gain or lose intrinsic soul mass. As one or more souls depart, other souls will enter.

Cuts are both shallow and deep, but care is taken to avoid the nervous system. Topical veins are often severed, though blood loss is expected to be minimal, and the circulatory system is considered only one of many target portals. Areas involving the human senses are standard access points. Cuts inside and around the ears are common, as are slits near the eyes and throat.

This period of readjustment may take days, during which the host may cycle through various types of catatonia, including deliria, mania, agitation, or paralysis. In an almost zombie-like state of living, most participants have no recollection of this time.

Hosts will be restrained to prevent them from harming their physical body, but the restraints, typically tied to saplings anchored in the walls, allow the necessary range of motion. It is in these physical clues that the physician understands what further steps to take. Wounds are reopened as required, and new incisions are common, although few compare to the number of initial cuts.

When the physician believes the acclimation is complete, the procedure is closed with a prayer. All wounds are dressed, and the host is placed in solitude for one to three days to allow the unconscious to bond with the conscious. Often the original personality disorder is replaced with a more subdued version of the same ailment, the Id, Ego, and Superego all remaining unchanged, just supported in a more harmonious way. The host is readmitted into society, and a small welcoming celebration for the host and the new souls are held. It is uncommon for hosts to undergo this procedure more than once, and only about five percent of a tribe's population will experience the treatment in their lifetime.

I witnessed one of these special events during my time in the Kongo. A young man, no more than thirteen, was deemed to have gravitated into mischievous ways and was recommended for adjustment. The tribal doctor, although conscious of the boy's declining nature decided to hold off on soul-transference until he was of a suitable age. I was allowed to observe the procedure. No laws prohibited such an audience, even from outside the tribe. Possibly because the tribe never had a need for such laws.

Manoka was not keen on watching the ceremony or participating in the celebratory ritual, but as my thirst for curiosity was welcomed, I strove to fit in as an outsider. The young man, Ntinu, was a willing participant, recognizing he needed help to remain in the tribe. He was washed and prepared while a group of twenty villagers sang a series of songs that I was unable to understand, but enjoyed through the uplifting melodies and rhythm.

The preparation lasted nearly an hour, during which time, the youth imbibed alcohol made from bananas, used as an anesthetic. Then the procedure started with the patient being laid on a table of comfortable cloths. The initial cuts seemed haphazard – one on the neck, the next on the inner thigh, the next in the armpit. The physician stroked like a mad painter, constantly reassessing the situation as if he could see the souls balancing in front of him.

Although many of the cuts were superficial and designed to avoid nerves, some pain was unavoidable as parts of the body were punctured, especially around the genitals and the underside of the feet. The bleeding appeared to be heavy, but, as the areas were routinely cleaned, I assessed the incisions were not life-threatening. The alcohol may have contributed to some thinning of his blood.

The cuts were not allowed to clot and block the souls' access points, so many were re-perforated. After no less than two-hundred perforations, the doctor stopped and said a small prayer. He motioned I should leave, at which time I returned to my camp, a three-minute walk from the center of the village.

Understanding my curiosity quite well, the physician later invited me to observe Ntinu in what appeared to be a seizure. He was restrained on the table by vines and saplings lashed to the structure of the dwelling. He was not comforted but rather left to thrash about on the table until he passed out from exhaustion. Though unconscious, his eyes gloped, as if staring the devil in the face. His mouth was closed, but his nostrils flared to pull oxygen from the air after this arduous attack.

When I returned later that evening, his eyes remained open and unblinking, though I believe he was still in an unconscious state. I was asked to leave him until morning, at which time he appeared to be carrying a low-grade fever. Some of his wounds oozed pus, which the physician attended to, removing the pus and cleaning the wound, but he applied no bandaging. I was particularly concerned about some of the slits so close to the young man's eyes and upon his privates, believing he could lose the function of those organs, but as a passive observer, I had no right to interfere or to suggest anything other than complete support for the physician's judgment.

Ntinu came out of the comatose state during the second night, and his wailing carried to my encampment. It was disconcerting to realize his distress, but alas, I could only pray he would make it through the night. When I visited him in the morning, his fever had advanced, and he was sweating through every pore on his body. Again, I feared for the boy's life.

Luckily, the fever broke, and he rested comfortably through the third night. Upon my next visit, he sat unrestrained on the table as the doctor dressed his many wounds. He was still not fully recovered mentally. The formerly outgoing boy, now mellowed, was led away to a segregated hut where he recuperated, eating small amounts of fruit and drinking water. Throughout the following two days, villagers stopped by and gave him short wishes through the window. By day three he spoke to them and thanked them, saying "*matondo*" which was a sign that he was gracious and raised well.

Before I left, Ntinu was released back to his household with a congratulatory celebration, and he swore he would have no more mischief.

I don't know how effective Ntinu's treatment was in the long term, but I was told it does not always work, and more drastic measures must be taken. I don't want to think about that. I'd rather believe in the thought that it *does* work, that soul-letting has been working for hundreds or even thousands of years, and there is no reason to think it any less of a viable treatment than today's modern medicine.

SPIDERMEN

Sixteen years ago, my wife, Katie, and I moved into a neighborhood on the outskirts of town. It was not an official retirement community, but we were one of the younger couples. And wow, those guys liked to party. There was always an occasion.

We arrived during peak holiday season, Halloween through New Year's Eve, and on top of formal holidays, we have happy hours, football parties, poker night, bingo night, and other random events to get everyone out of their houses. With so much going on, sometimes we'd decline from exhaustion, coming from a neighborhood where nobody talked to nobody, and most nights were spent sitting on the couch watching TV.

At one of the early events, I met Robert. We were out on the porch, chatting about what we did for a living and past experiences when a small, harmless-looking spider walked across Robert's face. I thought I might mention it, but Robert was already pretty drunk, so I figured he was desensitized to it. I was mesmerized as the spider wandered all over his face: on his eyelid, the bridge of his nose, over on the cheek, and even across his lips when he paused speaking.

I couldn't believe that a) he couldn't feel or see it no matter where it roamed, and b) it stayed for *so long*!

"Another beer?" Robert asked.

I nodded. "Sure."

He walked to the cooler and grabbed one for each of us, cracking his open. There were now *three* spiders on his face. At this point, I was at a loss for what to say. I mean, with one spider you can say, "Hey buddy, there's a spider on your face." Or you can say, "Who's your little friend?" and then tell them they have a small, harmless spider on their face. But when it gets to be more than one, and they're running around....

Eventually, I said my goodbyes, told him to enjoy the party, and went off to find Katie. I started to tell her about Robert, when she cut me off and said, "Oh yeah, he and his wife are shit-faced." I told her I agreed..., so much he didn't even know he had three spiders walking around on his face. She said that was gross and asked if I told him.

I said, "No, too awkward."

The next time I saw Robert he had a bandage on his cheek. I thought, *Oh dang, Robert got bit*. I asked him if he was alright. He said he cut himself shaving, and I was relieved. We were inside, so there were no bugs. We had an enjoyable conversation about boating, and I pictured him out on the boat, fishing, and flies all over his face as he was baiting the hook. He almost busted me chuckling to myself, but I covered it up with a story about Katie being attacked by a manta ray.

Speaking of flies, the next weekend we were at the park for a picnic. Big turnout, barbecue, and free beer. I met Robert's friend, Tom, who had lived in the neighborhood for about twenty years. Tom was in his late seventies and still enjoyed a beer or two, or more. We sat down at a table and a few flies were trying to peck at our food. As the group was carrying on about this and that, I looked over and Tom had two flies on his face.

Determined not to make the same mistake as with Robert, I told Tom, "You have two flies on your face." He said he didn't notice, and he waved them off, but they came right back. I would have expected him to wave them off again, but he didn't. It was super frustrating. Robert came over and the flies went to him too. It reminded me of the story of the Zuni Indians who had to sit naked on an anthill to become priests. I thought, *Robert and Tom would be good at that.*

This time Katie saw what I was seeing. She gave me an OMG look, and I rolled my eyes as if to say *what can you do?* At least I knew I wasn't imagining things.

Throughout the next year, especially the hot summer months, at picnics or the pool, we met more people who attracted bugs and didn't care.

Once, I was talking to a guy named Will, who had a mosquito feasting on a big, fat vein on the top of his head. I wanted to smack that greedy, plump glutton so hard. The thing could barely fly; it was so fat. And then there was George, who had some type of small mites (maybe fleas?) crawling all in and around his ears and the hair sticking out of them.

I began to think this was what I was going to be resigned to... living out my senior years with bugs scurrying all over my face, and I wouldn't even care. This went on for two more years, and I never got used to the pervasiveness of this pestilence. It seemed to be only here, at Lakeland.

Not everyone was affected. I asked my friend Brian, who never had spiders or flies on him, if he had noticed. He hadn't, but a week later, he pulled me aside at a function and said Walt had a ladybug under his cheekbone near the corner of his mouth. He couldn't believe it. Now, Walt has really high, bony cheekbones, so it's believable he couldn't see the damned thing, but not being able to feel it is another story.

Brian and I became the secret police for bug sightings. We recruited Paul, who we had also vetted as having never had bugs on his face. Katie was an unofficial member of our group and was on the lookout for any of her lady friends with this malady. We started documenting which people had which bugs, and how many times, to establish a pattern.

I called up my friend Jordan, an entomologist for a chemical company. He said drinking beer and sweating could attract insects, and some people sweat more or drink more than average. *Hmmm. These guys did both.*

But attracting bugs was only half of the equation. Not doing anything about it was the other. Either they couldn't feel them, or they didn't care.

Brian's son, a neurology intern, said the desensitization could point to an underlying medical condition like multiple sclerosis or diabetes, but those afflictions aren't communicable. As a stretch, a minute percentage of people suffer from HSN2 (hereditary sensory neuropathy type 2) in which they can't feel pain or pressure or temperature. But it's likely genetic. Our neighbors grew up all over the country.

We were at a loss.

I made the mistake of bringing it up with Judy, who was married to our neighbor, Greg.

Greg already had tick marks on our roster (pun intended, that's what we jokingly called them) for separate incidents of mosquitos and a dragonfly(!). When a yellow jacket landed on his neck, I caught Judy signaling to him by using her middle finger on her own neck. He brushed it away, but it was soon back, and she repeated the gesture. Later, I joked with her that wasps must really like Greg… they kept coming back and back, and he never got stung.

She played it off, "He just has that effect on bugs. I can go out and never see one, but I come in all bitten up, and Greg never gets anything, though they're all around him."

"Why do you think that is?" I asked.

She knew I was probing and ended it abruptly, "I don't know." Then much more cheerfully, "I should see if anyone needs more wine!"

She was whispering to Greg later, and it had to be about me busting their little charade, but I moved out of earshot to indicate I wasn't eavesdropping.

I reported back to the Jameson Club, which is what nicknamed ourselves, based on the fictional character JJ Jameson, Spiderman's employer at the Daily Bugle who was always trying to discover Spiderman's secret identity. We also drank Jameson whiskey as a cover in case it ever came out in public. Once it did come out, and Frank, who was frequently visited by flies and gnats by the droves, said he wanted to come drink with us. Whenever Frank joined us we met indoors, so we could keep straight faces.

I told the guys and Katie how Judy was being evasive when I busted her signing with Greg. She had to be in on it, and if she was, probably so were some of the other wives.

To test the theory, we planned a party at our house. It was shortly after Memorial Day, when the humidity spikes, welcoming bugs in full force. A couple of men from our Jameson Club Hall of Fame declined, which was disappointing, but we still had a pretty good turnout, and we caught three of the wives flashing signs to the husbands on our list. Betty wiped her bangs, Charlene adjusted her earring, and Vernie smiled unnaturally: she must have been new at it.

We could now tell there was some serious collusion, but this knowledge went both ways. We were considered outsiders, the unafflicted few among the many, and the old saying *"If you're not in, you're out"* applied to us.

After a while, the spidermen started to decline some of our invitations or steer clear at outdoor gatherings. It was noticeable. So, the Jameson Club hatched a plan to break the case: a threefold attack with ultimately good intentions: infiltrate the group, expose the secret, and get some help for these poor people.

The perfect opportunity arose when my old boss, Larry, decided to move to Lakeland. I let him in on the secret after he bought his house and was committed to the move. He and I had done some crazy stuff traveling together over the years, so I knew I could trust him, and he'd like the challenge.

He sampled various perfumes and soaps in an effort to attract bugs to his face, but he kept getting bit. Ultimately,

K-Y desensitizing gel did the trick. The bugs loved it, and he couldn't feel a thing! It even had a pleasant, but muted scent which he didn't mind. We didn't let Larry's wife Julie in on the secret, though. We wanted her reaction to be genuine.

We rolled out our plan at the next big event, and since we kept our relationship a secret, no one was blackballing Larry yet. He was free to roam around and make new friends.

Larry was a hit with the spidermen, but as he let the flies graze on his face, Julie fanned them away more than once. I told Brian, "It's going down."

Julie got pulled aside by Betty, and they talked for a sec before Betty returned to the group. Julie wandered over to the dessert table alone, started swatting at the desserts, and then told Larry she'd wait for him in the car. They needed to *go*.

According to Larry, Betty told Julie the flies and other insects at Lakeland were very friendly and never bit anyone. Julie thought Betty was senile, and told Larry he needed to use extra-strength bug spray next time they went to an outdoor function: this place had too many bugs. There was no secret invitation offered, so we were disappointed.

But we kept up the charade at a few more events, and a couple of months later, on the golf course, Frank pulled Larry aside and asked him if the number of bugs at Lakeland was bothering him. Larry played it off like a pro, saying they were harmless.

Frank said, "You know, these little buggers will help us live longer than the others. They deposit some of the native plants into the skin, and you won't age as rapidly. Some of us guys use a moisturizer they like, and we never get bit. We even have an unofficial club, and I've been asked to invite you.

"You can't tell guys not in the club, but you know some of them: Brian and Paul and Patrick. If you ever tell—" He changed his tone, thinking he'd attract more bees with honey, "Well, we'd love to have you around."

Larry wasn't scared of the old man's threat, so he told us right away, but we weren't sure what to do with the information. Larry was content to let it play out for a while, although Julie caught him putting on K-Y before a party at the Bergman house.

That's when they told him about FlySafe. The gel most of the guys used, was a moisturizer invented by Bernie's son, a PhD chemist. The lotion had a scent bugs dug and made humans non-threatening, thereby preventing bites and stings. Later we learned it was also visible under ultraviolet light.

Three more years went by, and Larry secretly kept us up-to-date on the Scarab Club, the name they had coined based on the ancient Egyptians' reverence for the dung beetle.

Relations with the spidermen were still cordial, but we were ostracized in some social settings. I liked Frank and Tom and Greg, and the others, and I hated being blackballed, but what could I do?

I ran it by Larry. "What would happen if I came up to the group of y'all and demanded to be let in on the little secret?"

"We'd deny it."

"Well, what if I told them I knew all about their special lotion and swore to keep it to myself?"

"First, they'd probably know it was me who told you, and I'd be kicked out or something worse. Second, if they didn't find out it was me, do you really want to start this lifestyle just to hang out with a bunch of old guys and alie—" He stopped like he had just had a mini-stroke.

I ignored it. "Maybe *we* should just move away. There are other neighborhoods."

"But you like it here and moving is a pain in the ass."

I was worn out. "So what then?"

"You know Ned?"

"Yeah, the guy who lives by himself?"

"Yep. Well, he's lived here almost as long as you, and suddenly he was in." The spidermen accepted him even though he never previously exhibited an affinity for the insects. Larry suspected he had been tipped on FlySafe and was now using it. He suggested I could use it too. He rubbed his face and said, "It works. I'm younger-looking than when I got here."

I suspected FlySafe was giving him dementia. "I'll talk it over with Katie. I don't think she'll like it. She'd rather move."

"That's what Julie said too, but the ladies convinced her to stay. They use the lotion, too. In other ways," he said with a wink. "And... there's another side effect I never mentioned. It puts a little more steel in your sword, if you know what I mean…." Wink number two. "I can have Julie talk to Katie, if you're serious."

That was ten years ago. Katie and I have never been happier, and now we have no holes in our friendship circle. Paul and Brian were admitted into the Scarab Club around the same time as the neighborhood women and there's no one here not on the "stuff." We have an aggressive weeding-out process for vetting prospective homeowners before they move in. It involves some strategically placed nests.

All this time it was a big misunderstanding. I thought the Scarab Club members had early onset dementia, maybe from the use of FlySafe, but it turns out they discovered that the insects were really aliens from another galaxy. There's no other way to explain why our neighborhood is so unique and why we are all getting younger.

POOL SNAKES

"Now, Trina, hear me out…." Demetrius was sure he had found a compromise she couldn't refuse. "It's *not* camping. It's a cabin. And it's got TV's, and a big kitchen, and a pool…. See?" He handed the phone to her with pictures of a beautiful A-frame nestled in the woods with giant trees all around.

Trina was a city girl, but this *did* look Instagram-worthy. And she could show D she was a team player.

Demetrius was still trying to sell it. "We could teach Ana to swim…."

"Alright, D. Enough, I'm in."

Demetrius jumped back with both fists pumped. "Yeah!" He took the phone from Trina. "I'm booking it now 'fore you change your mind." He had the best memories camping with his uncle and aunt in northwest Arkansas when he was a little boy. Now, living in St. Louis, he was always trying to get Trina to escape the city and "embrace nature," but she'd been reluctant. *Maybe even obstinate.*

Trina had the opposite experience. At summer camp between first and second grade, they had seen a live scorpion and a dead baby rattlesnake. The other girls thought it was cool, but little Catrina cried until the camp counselor allowed her to call her mom. She didn't get the emotional support she was expecting, though. Momma Wright told her, "Relax and suck it up, baby. I'll pick you up in five days." Trina spent as much of the week as she could in the cabin, in the top bunk, playing her Gameboy.

She told D in no uncertain terms that she was not going to get in a tent and sleep on the dirt. "Who knows what could crawl in there at night?" Demetrius put his dream on hold for a while, but now, he had found a compromise.

#

All packed up, with the Nissan Rogue overflowing with "essentials," Demetrius had to help the automatic hatch close the last two inches. He shook his head. He liked the simplicity of a tent, a fishing pole, tackle box, and a box of matches. *Pick up some beer on the way.* Trina packed like she and Ana Mae were going to live in Europe for a month. But if "glamping" was a way to introduce the two of them to the serenity and peacefulness of the outdoors, then so be it.

They took the interstate south toward the Ozarks and into northern Arkansas. The place he had picked out was only about twenty miles from where he had camped as a kid, in the middle of a dense forest near a river. It was only about five miles out of town, so they could get food and drinks whenever they needed it.

As they pulled off the road, Trina was a little hesitant to see the dirt road disappearing into tree cover. "Are you sure this is it, D? I don't wanna get shot out here, trespassing on someone's property."

Ana Mae chimed in from the backseat, "Me either."

Demetrius said, "No one's getting shot. I've got the directions, and we're right where we're supposed to be." And not ten seconds later, the trees cleared, and the gorgeous house appeared as the clearing opened up before them.

"Whoa." Ana Mae's eyes sparkled. "It looks like a giant treehouse!" Trina and Demetrius hadn't shared any photos of the property with Ana, and she was amazed by its size and shape. Trina smiled at D. *He did good.* It was even better looking than on the website. And inside it was amazing. Beautiful furniture they couldn't afford for their own house, and airy, with lots of vertical space, and floor to ceiling windows on the backside that let the outdoors in. And it was spotless. No scorpions or other bugs to be found anywhere.

"Daddy, is my room upstairs?" Ana Mae looked up to the loft area at the top of the tall spiral wooden staircase.

"You bet! I think we're all up there," Demetrius said, remembering the layout from the online photos.

"Let's go look!" Ana grabbed his hand and pulled him up the stairs.

Demetrius smiled inside. *Both his girls were happy. This was going great.*

After Ana Mae picked her room from the two options, and they all unloaded the car, they traveled into town to get groceries. The small market had everything they needed to stock up on for their adventure. Demetrius bought a couple of cheap floats, and pool noodles that Ana called snakes.

At checkout, the clerk asked, "You guys staying at the Miller's place? Big A-Frame in the woods about two miles that way?"

"Ah yes," Demetrius nodded and pointed at the clerk, remembering the welcome note from the Millers. "I booked it online, so I didn't meet them in person."

"Nice folks. Great place, but you're gonna need this." She grabbed four huge cans of bug spray from behind the counter and rang it up like there was no option. Demetrius looked at Trina like, *"Okay... makes sense...ring it up."* Trina looked at Demetrius like, *"That many bugs? That's a lot of bugs."*

When they got back, Trina started to put away the groceries, and Demetrius and Ana Mae decided to check out the backyard. He wanted to make sure the grill was working and ensure the pool was clean. The grill was hooked up to the gas from the house, and he didn't need the charcoal he bought. He turned it on, clicked the lighter, and it fired right up. *Nice...way better than home. Steaks tonight.*

Ana Mae stood several feet back from the pool's edge. "Daddy, there's no shallow part."

True, the kidney shaped pool didn't even have steps. Just a ladder on either side. But it was only four feet deep on the left end. "Don't worry, you're gonna have your water wings, and by the time we leave here, you're gonna swim like *The Little Mermaid*."

"Ariel."

"Yup, her. Let's go check up on your momma."

Trina had all the food put away and was already enjoying a glass of red wine. "How were the bugs?"

"Not a bug in sight, but maybe it's too hot right now. I saw some Tiki torches and about ten bottles of citronella, so, later I'll put those out, and they'll keep the mosquitos away. And we still have four *giant* cans of bug spray, so I think we're good."

"Okay, if you say so. Imma sit right here in the AC and drink my wine and read my book."

"We're gonna hit the pool. Ana, baby, go upstairs and put on your swimsuit, and Daddy will go get his and we can try the short end of the pool."

"Momma, the pool doesn't have any steps."

Trina shot a glance at her husband. *Strike one, you know she's scared of pools.* But then to Ana, "Daddy will be there. And you got your water wings and the floats and the pool snakes. You'll be fine. I'll watch you from the window."

That seemed to work, and Ana left to get her suit on.

"D, you know she gets scared after what happened at the Williams'."

"It's been a year and a half. She'll get over it. Just needs to get some confidence and then she'll be fine."

"Hope you're right. I'll be here, listening to her screams…good thing there's no neighbors…"

#

It was a standoff. Demetrius in the shallow end of the pool and Ana Mae in her pink and white *Little Mermaid* swimsuit with one blow-up water wing around each upper arm, not wanting to jump in.

Finally, Demetrius gave in and said, "Baby, just sit on the side and put your feet in the water. You don't have to get in today."

But Ana was reluctant to do even that. *What if she slipped and fell in like she did at Keisha's house last year?*

111

Demetrius pulled himself out of the water on the side, not using the ladder and sat on the edge. "Come here, baby girl."

Ana joined him and found it was okay to sit. The water was splashy, and she moved both her feet together like a mermaid tail. They looked out at the trees past the pool and tried to name as many animals in the forest as they could.

"Spiders."

"Snakes."

"Wolf."

"Monkey."

"Ha ha, Daddy. There's no monkeys in there. Monkeys live in the jungle."

"What about the Arkansas Vampire Monkeys?" and Demetrius tickled Ana all over....

Trina looked out the window and smiled. She was glad D hadn't forced Ana to get in the pool. This vacation was already a hundred times better than she thought it would be. *No work. Just relax. Maybe one more wine…*

#

Demetrius made some delicious steaks, and Ana selected mac and cheese as a side. Ana helped her dad light the tiki torches, and they had ten of them surrounding the lawn area around the pool. They ate on the porch, and though everything smelled like bug spray, they didn't get bit at all.

They heard a coyote or wolf (as Ana called it) somewhere in a canyon far away. Otherwise it was just the sound of crickets and the hum of the pool equipment.

#

The next day, Demetrius planned a hike into the woods. Ana wanted to go, but Trina was not so adventurous. She said she was happy to hang back and read her book. "Don't go too far."

Ana had never seen so many tall trees, and they found a lot of insects, squirrels, and even a raccoon. At the edge of the clearing, just before they stepped into the backyard, a garter snake slithered across their path.

Ana squealed, but Demetrius told her, "That's a garter snake. They're friendly, and they only eat bugs. They don't bite. See his head? It's the same size as his body. That means he doesn't have poison sacs in his cheeks."

Ana said, "We should catch him and put him in a box and feed him insects from the woods. And show mommy."

Luckily for Trina (and Demtrius), the snake was a little too fast, and they couldn't catch it. Trina would have whooped his ass if he'd brought that thing into the house.

After a family nap, they played outside. Demetrius found a sprinkler and hooked it up to the hose for Ana Mae to run through while he and Trina floated in the pool on their blow-up rafts. *The Millers know what's up,* D thought. *Maybe this was a place they could come back to year after year.*

Trina was thinking the same thing with her happy child and her husband there. No stress. Easy living. So relaxed, she drifted off to sleep.

Demetrius got out of the pool and dried off Ana. He took her inside and made sure she took a shower. He let Trina just float in the pool. He'd wake her up when he started the grill for dinner. *Barbecue chicken...*

#

Trina was dreaming she was laying on a beach in the Caribbean. The breeze and the sun were perfect. She didn't see the garter snake sliding into the pool or the water moccasin following it.

#

Ana walked down the staircase. Playing in the sprinkler was fun. Better than the pool. She had gotten dressed, but no one was downstairs. Maybe they were outside. With some effort, she pulled open the sliding glass door to the porch. *Mommy was still in the pool but so were about two dozen snakes. Guarder snakes. That's what Daddy called them. Mommy would be okay. But there was one, no two, no* three *of the bad snakes Daddy said had big heads. And one of them ate the Guarder snake! And one was about to eat Mommy!*

"Mommy, wake up!" Ana screamed at the pool and ran down the steps. Demetrius heard her from inside and bounded down the steps in his underwear. Trina opened her eyes to see that she was surrounded by snakes of every size and color. She started to go into shock. Some of the snakes had made their way up onto the raft. The small kidney-shaped pool was filled with them.

Ana saw the snakes on her mom were just the garter snakes. She forgot she was afraid of the water and jumped in. She wasn't swimming, but she wasn't drowning either as she grabbed the raft and started pulling the snakes off her mom, who was starting to jerk away from the snakes, but was not leaving the raft.

Demetrius flew down the porch steps to the pool and took inventory of the scene. *Cottonmouth 12 o'clock, 3 o'clock, 6 o'clock. Too many garter snakes to count. Child in the pool who can't swim, but was holding on to the raft. Trina thrashing on the raft at her wits end.* He grabbed the pool net and wrangled out the water moccasin closest to Trina. He yelled at her, "Get under water! Swim to the ladder!" but she wouldn't move.

One cottonmouth was closing in on Ana Mae, who was still grabbing the harmless water snakes off Trina. She was the next priority. "Ana, grab the pole!" He reached it out in front of her, but she refused.

"Momma needs me," Ana shouted above the splashing, and now screaming, Trina.

Demetrius saw an opening. Snagging the 6 o'clock cottonmouth and throwing him over to the 3 o'clock one, he jumped in and pushed the raft with Trina, Ana Mae, and two dozen garters off to the shallow end. He grabbed Ana and put her on the side and slung Trina over his shoulder, climbing the ladder out of the pool. Demitrius carried Trina up to the top deck, laid her down on the chaise lounge and returned to the pool.

He yelled at Ana Mae to go help her mom and emptied all the unused lighter fluid and torch fuel into the pool and lit it up. The pool was instantly ablaze with burning snakes, most importantly the three cottonmouths. Three snakes tried to slither up the porch steps, but Demetrius was in Rambo-mode. He grabbed a can of bug spray, pressed the button and lit it, directing the homemade flamethrower at the invading reptiles that could not escape his wrath.

Trina was in a stupor. Ana and Demetrius tried to get through to her, but her brain was in lockdown. The fire in the pool burned out, and they guided Trina to the car, where she sat in a catatonic state while Demetrius ran back in and dressed.

#

After a heavily sedated overnight stay at the hospital, Trina was mostly back to herself the next morning. She had no memory of the traumatic event. Demetrius told Ana he thought it best to keep it their little secret. They told Trina she may have had "too much sun" and left it at that. The Millers generously refunded the Walkers for their stay and offered an invitation to return anytime, but Demetrius politely declined. Next year they were going to New York City.

Ana Mae spent the rest of the summer at the neighborhood pool, and by the end of August she could swim across the whole width without water wings. Trina told her she swam like a fish, but Ana said, "More like a Guarder snake," and cheesily smiled at her dad.

"Smells like rain," I said aloud as we stepped out of the van into the warm Indian air.

"Oh, yes, Mr. Ferris. This is Kalbaisakhi season," Arvand said. "Big storms. Big wind."

Just then, a small gust caught us from behind. He smiled at me and said, "No. Bigger."

I entered the expansive building, where workers were assembling and packing out my high-end line of binoculars. I was exceptionally pleased with this factory. We had developed leaders in every department and produced some of the highest quality products of any facility in the world. The equipment was well-maintained, and the people were self-directed. Through managing costs, we improved the facilities, added a breakroom, paid well above nominal wages, and built a culture of trust and family.

Based on the frequent and accurate reports the factory gave me on the progress, I didn't have to be there during the rainy season, but I didn't want to be a ghost owner. I wanted to be invested in my people as much as I wanted them to be invested in my products.

I came to India four years prior, looking for die casting and plastic molding. At a tradeshow, I met Arvand, who guaranteed I could source components from local suppliers in West Bengal and save exorbitant supply chain markups. I needed some convincing, so I did a trial run of inexpensive magnifying rings and was pleased with his responsiveness and ability to manage costs and quality.

After nine months in Kolkata, I introduced higher-end products: golf rangefinders and rifle scopes. I started a second plant 175 miles away in Jamshedpur and another in between, in Kharagpur.

I still tried to avoid the rainy season June to September, but visited at least twice a year. It was a great place to escape the freezing mid-western winters in the US.

Now, hearing about the *kalbaisakhis* in April, I was thinking I should widen my personal rain embargo a couple of months.

I finished up a meeting with the Kharagpur factory leads on our first quarter results and growth plans when the roof rattled above us. Several workers were checking the weather on their phones and Arvand approached me. "Looks like we will have a nor'wester the next three days. We may have to move the glass."

I was not happy about halting production, but it was the right thing to do. We had built special storage units with heavy-duty doors at each site to store the most valuable components. As a precaution against the impending storm, we moved the lenses to these all-concrete storerooms where they'd be safest from rain and wind. The employees would continue on the plastic and metal housings for a few more hours.

I had to laugh that the locals called it a "nor-wester." They sounded like they had seen one too many American movies, the slang sounding foreign to my adopted ears.

The gales picked up as Arvind drove me to my hotel, two miles down the same road as the factory. Arvand said to watch the TV, and he would keep me updated on all three locations.

Around 9 p.m., Arvand called to report hail falling on Jamshedpur, one hundred miles away. The good news was that Jamshedpur, at the front end, was in the least danger. The storm would accumulate over time. In Kharagpur, we were already getting rain, and the wind was picking up as the trees outside my hotel window bowed to the east.

The DD India TV broadcast monitored the kalbaisakhi as it progressed across eastern India. They depicted the 250-mile sheer line, as it moved like a wave toward the coast.

We had these gusts of wind back home in northeast Oklahoma. Though we were situated outside the famous Tornado Alley, pressure systems caused wind sheers, called *derechos*, to race across the plain toward Arkansas and Missouri. The gale-force winds were often accompanied by thunderstorms and hail, and often knocked out power. We were a lot more scared of tornadoes than derechos, but both carried danger to anyone or anything exposed.

This kalbaisakhi was like a mega-derecho, ready to whoop up on India and neighboring Bangladesh, and we just had to wait it out.

The first storm hit Kharagpur about two in the morning. Hail attacked the windows, and the wind whistled around the building, a modern international hotel that had to be one of the safest places in the city. I was worried for our factory and its sheet metal roof. One time the roof of a Walmart in Bentonville, Arkansas got ripped off by a derecho and parts of it fell into the aisles.

Despite the time, I texted Arvind to get an idea if this was a normal-sized version of one of these storms. He replied, "Sir, this one looks pretty bad. Please stay where you are." And then, "If it seems like it has passed, more will come. Storm not done."

I wasn't planning to go anywhere. My hotel had food and safety, but I was worried about my workers, many of whom lived in modest houses or apartments near the factories. The storm intensified over the next few hours. Tree limbs the size of a car blew by. I decided to stay back from the window, not knowing if one was going to come crashing through. The TV showed intense rainfall right where I was. *Yup, confirmed.*

By morning, the rain was lessening, and the wind had died down to a few gusts here and there. My cell phone didn't work. I called the front desk, and they said mobile towers in the area were down. They suggested wi-fi calling if the other party had internet access. I texted my factory leads to check on their families. Jayshree in Kolkata confirmed her family was okay, the storm had turned farther south to Digha. JJ in Jamshedpur said it was still "quite windy" and offered to contact the Kharagpur staff since I had not yet reached Arvind, whose last text had been, "Kharagpur very bad."

I was starting to feel a sense of dread. Smallest site, building most susceptible to disaster, and we couldn't reach anyone. I was sure they were okay.... They were more used to this than I was, but it didn't stop my mind from racing to the worst conclusions.

Over the next hour we found out several of the workers were unreachable. The local police said the area around the factory was hit especially hard, and they couldn't approach the area. Across the city, many people had been pulled from raging flood waters, and a few were pronounced dead.

Around 9 a.m. the winds and rain subsided. Arvind finally texted back. I told him several employees were missing. "I might have to go check."

He responded, "Storm not done. Will call you." He wi-fi called me to tell me more storms were imminent and perhaps worse than the original. I asked him what we could do.

He answered my question with the same question. He said, "Mr. Ferris, what could *you* do?" I didn't know. I was a stranger with little knowledge of the area or the language or the customs. I was just a guy trying to make sure my factory family was safe.

By 10 a.m. the wind was calm. The factory was only two miles away. I decided I'd go out and find them.

I walked down the back stairs (they'd never have let me out of the lobby) and into a slight rainfall. Barely a spring shower.... What we in Oklahoma call "spitting."

The water was waist-deep in places, and at one low-water crossing, I lost my footing and had to swim across. The effluent was opaque, light brown, and smelly. I tried to push away thoughts that it contained animal and maybe human waste. Got a little in my mouth and spent two minutes puh-puhing it off my lips and gums. I was hoping for a little *more* rain to cleanse the filthy runoff I was covered in.

I reached higher ground and wound my way past a grove of trees and into the wide-open and decimated industrial park. Roof metal lay strewn across the complex, and I saw no sign of life. It was like a tornado had touched down, despite no reports of one. The dark skies started to empty, and the wind picked up again. I thought of Arvind's "Storm not done" text.

I rounded the corner of the Onlexx Corporation's building where a section of wall was missing. We used Onlexx to make the cardboard inserts for some of our packaging. I peered inside and called out in case someone was trapped. The floor was flooded but the room was empty.

Relieved for only a moment, I went back outside to see a piece of sheet metal moving. A man, face down on the gravel lot, struggled as a large roofing sheet had sunk into the back of his leg, severing his hamstrings. He cried out for help, and I realized what Arvind meant. I'm not a doctor; I had no vehicle or phone service. I couldn't communicate… *What could* I *do?*

The roof section embedded into his leg was keeping him from bleeding to death. I dared not remove it. I motioned to him that I would go for help. I doubt he understood my pantomimes, but he reached forward to give me his phone. He had called 112 a dozen times. We had no signal on either of our phones. I gave him the phone back and told him in English, "I'll be back." He wailed the most heart wrenching cry as I left him to find my team.

The rain was pouring now, and more metal was starting to fly around. I felt like I was in the bottom of a blender with the blades about to slice me in half any second. Several times I was struck by flying branches, but luckily no tin roof sections flew near me. I stuck to the leeward side of the Onlexx building as long as possible. My building was a hundred feet away.

Only the OPES from FERRIS SCOPES still remained on the building. The doors were blown wide open, and I knew the roof was gone. Unfortunately, four cars were still there, smashed to hell. It appeared not everyone had left the office park.

I picked up a piece of plywood as a shield and dashed across the span between Onlexx and my building. The wind caught the plywood and lifted me clear off the ground. I flew twenty feet before the plywood was ripped from my hand, and I landed on my right shoulder to the crack of my collarbone. In seventh grade, I broke my collarbone playing football at recess, so I knew what it was right away. There was nothing I could do; you can't splint a collarbone.

I got up, heading straight into the wind and rain, and through God's graces, I did not get murdered. The factory floor was a mess. All the tables and equipment were pinned against the east wall and the floor was full of debris from the surrounding buildings and forest. Only a small piece of the roof remained, and it was shaking its way loose from its bolts. I couldn't be around when it broke free.

I dodged into the mostly intact office, which still had all of its plexiglass walls, when the roof piece sailed through the building and smashed into the concrete wall next to the office, buckling in half and leaving a three-foot scrape. Thirty seconds earlier and I might have been decapitated.

The rain was coming down inside the factory now. If the employees were here, they would surely be in the storage bunkers with the lenses. *But wouldn't they have left when the first rain subsided?*

I found a ring of keys in the office corner and dashed out the door at the end of the factory floor. In the maelstrom, I struggled to find the right key. The ring had more than twenty keys on it, and I kept losing my place as the rain and wind buffeted me. I was calling out but couldn't hear anything above the howling.

I got the door a quarter of the way open, and it blew back against the building, nearly taking me out. I pulled on the door with all my might and couldn't get it to close against the wind. The lenses were inside, but no employees. I had to try the second unit.

Now knowing what the keys looked like, I quicky unlocked the second unit. I turned the handle and carefully opened the door, not wanting it to blow open permanently. A face peered out. It was Pravind, the site manager. "Oh my god, Mr. Ferris, sir. Thank you." He helped me into the small room and shut the door, but not before putting a slice of cardboard in the opening and explaining, "The lock cannot be opened from the inside. We have been locked in here."

There were two other men and two women in the small room. One woman was barely conscious.

"Mr. Ferris, sir. Why are you here? It is very dangerous out there."

"You were missing. We needed to know if you were okay."

"Maya has lost a lot of blood." Maya, one of our top assemblers had a tourniquet around her forearm and another bandage around her wrist. She was sleeping. Pravind said her hand was completely severed at the wrist, and she would lose the hand if she didn't receive immediate medical attention. And maybe even if she did.

We couldn't go back out. The wind and rain had intensified. The bunker was solid. I was sure the optics in the now-open unit would soon be destroyed, but that was a secondary concern. When the new storm subsided in a few hours, we could try to leave.

I hired Pravind, but I didn't know much about him or the others in the bunker, other than recognizing their "off the charts" dedication to the job. We kept each other's spirits up by discussing our families, our hobbies, and our long-term plans. Pravind had visited the US several times and once even drove Route 66 through Oklahoma. We might have been a few miles from each other and not have known it.

After two and a half hours, the rain and wind lessened. We weren't going to be able to drive, with low-water crossings in both directions, but we had to find medical care for Maya ASAP. The best chance was to walk back toward my hotel.

Although a bit unsteady on her feet, Maya led us out of the shelter. She was resigned to the possibility that her hand might be lost forever, if not her lower arm, but she wasn't going to sit around and do nothing.

The man in the parking lot was deceased. We moved him inside the warehouse office and placed a tarp over him.

Later we spotted a couple of wild dogs near the main road looking for food. He'd be safe in the office until the authorities arrived.

We didn't scour the rest of the business park for other survivors, and our shouts were unanswered. We headed south, back to the ravine, which was even more raging and brown than when I first crossed.

Dilip, one of our younger assemblers, raced up the stream and found us a safer place to cross. We only got wet up to our waists, and Maya was able to keep her hand out of the water. We made it into town just as the third front rolled in.

The wind pushed us toward the hotel. Branches and sleet buffeted us from behind. We dodged into a carport for some relief, but it would have been better to continue to the hotel because this storm was the worst of the three.

Signposts sailed through the air like axes, and the electrical line across the street crashed to the ground with fiery sparks. I was worried the water between the downed lines and the carport would electrocute us, and I held my breath expecting to be fried. The power must have cut off immediately because we were spared as the light from the hotel sign and roof lights went out. Though it was four in the afternoon, it was black as night with the grid down.

A door led from the carport to the building, but it was solidly locked, and we had no way to bash it in. We huddled together as close to the center of the wall as we could. Maya was starting to sweat, and I was concerned she was going into shock.

Dilip volunteered to try to commandeer a van from the hotel. Not waiting for acceptance, he ran across the street as the reserve power came on. He went stiff as a board and fell face forward. The rushing water carried him toward the hotel, out of our sight. He had to have had the poor timing to step on a wire at the wrong moment. I went after him.

I kept to the right side of the street away from the power line and found Dilip unconscious but with a pulse. I picked up the frail boy, no more than seventeen years old, and carried him another half-block to the hotel lobby, hastily unlocked by the night manager who had never left.

A nurse and a doctor staying at the hotel attended to Dilip while I went back for the others, but Pravind was already escorting the rest of the group into the lobby. Maya's bandages were redone properly, though she would still lose her lower arm.

Dilip and Maya weathered the next four hours, and as soon as possible were transported to the South Eastern Railway Main Hospital, which was deluged with patients. Dilip was released the next day. Maya had an operation and was released in a week. My collarbone healed in a couple of months, but sometimes aches in cold weather. Gives me a reason to go back to India. Maya returned to Ferris after only two weeks of recovery, even though I offered her disability time for eight. She transferred into the quality inspection group, became a lead, and worked for me for another twenty years.

After my recommendation (and perhaps a small endowment), IIT Kharagpur offered Dilip a scholarship in Civil Engineering. His company, Boishakh Solutions, specializes in safe, low-cost, rural buildings and has over six hundred patents.

Arvind Ashgara bought Ferris Optics from me three years ago, allowing me to retire. He might have been the only person I would have sold to. Other than the new president, and one of my best friends in the world, Pravind Gopal.

LITTLE RED WAGON

I was very close to my grandpa. He understood me in a way that others who spent more time with me did not. He wore warm sweaters and told knock-knock jokes, and he loved to read books with me and make me ice cream shakes. That's why I was so upset when he passed away. He was old, and both of us knew it would eventually happen, but we never spoke about it. We didn't have to talk about things we both knew.

I grieved in my room, with my stuffed animals, and slept a lot. Mom and Dad were concerned, but they didn't try to push me too hard. After the funeral, Mom came to my room and said that Grandpa had left me a letter:

Dearest Chloe,

You have always been the person who I wanted to spend time with more than any other. If you're getting this, it means that I have hopefully ended up in heaven after a long, full life. Please don't worry about me. But I do want you to know that if I can, I will come back and check on you from time to time. Tell your mom to leave the little red wagon in your yard. If I come back as an animal I will sit in the little red wagon, and you will know it's me.

Love,

Grandpa

I went out to the backyard, and my wagon was right where I had left it, near the shed. There were no squirrels or birds or even insects in it, but I got some cleaner from Mom and shined it up really well. Then I sat on the porch and waited for anything to jump in for a ride, but nothing came, and finally I had to go inside.

Day after day I sat on the porch, hoping to see my Grandpa come back to check on me like he'd promised, but as time went by, I figured that maybe he was not able to come back and visit me after all. I wasn't mad at him; I knew if he could have come back he would have. Years passed, and I moved away for college and started a family of my own. My mom gave me the red wagon for my kids to play with, and I had mixed feelings about it. It was a source of hope and disappointment at the same time, but disappointment is fleeting, and hope is eternal, so I kept it. I even looked out at it in the backyard from time to time like I did as a kid, hoping to find a small creature sitting in it, staring back at me.

My kids liked the wagon when they were young. My five-year-old daughter, Gracy, would pull my four-year-old son, Michael, to take him fake shopping around the yard. I got lots of cute pictures of them, and the wagon reclaimed its significance in my life. Time went on, and eventually my parents passed away. As I was going through their things, I found some old photos of our family and even older ones of Grandpa. In one of them, my grandpa, as a small boy, was riding in a similar wagon to ours. And the photo, though black and white and grainy, looked eerily similar to the photos I had of Michael, who was now a tax attorney.

I went to my computer and pulled up the photos from when Michael was a toddler, and there he was, grinning at the camera the same way Grandpa was in the old photo from the 1930's. I printed it, and after Christmas dinner with Michael and his family, I showed him the two pictures side by side. He looked at me in bewilderment and said in a perfect impersonation of Grandpa, "Yes, Chloe, didn't you get my letter?"

"Why don't you just go talk to her?"

"What?" I wasn't paying attention, then realized what Jo said. "Her? No way."

"She's just a person like you and me."

"Um, no she's not." The girl on the dance floor with the long brown hair to her waist and the absolutely perfect face and body had been monopolizing my time the past thirty minutes, and I couldn't tear my eyes away. Unless she looked in my direction. Then I stared at my drink hoping she didn't catch my head jerking away.

"You know, she keeps looking over here."

"Yeah, I think she busted me staring at her. I'm getting another drink, want one?"

"Nah, I'm good. I'm gonna see what Nate's up to." Nate was in the back area of the bar playing pool with his buddies. My sister, Jo, and Nate had been dating for two years. They were past the awkward stage, comfortable being together or apart. Tonight, she was trying to be my "wingman." I was usually a "third wheel" on weekends, and I think she felt sorry for me.

I spotted an opening at the crowded bar and made a beeline for it, hoping to be recognized in the next ten minutes for a refresher. I wasn't assertive—not with girls, not with getting what I wanted, not with life in general.

Clearly, above the loud music, I heard, "Hey, can we get a drink over here?"

The bartender, "Julian" stopped what he was doing and looked past me to the tall girl who I'd been fixated on. She was right behind me. "He's been here for a while." And she pointed to me.

I was flustered to be getting attention in two directions, and I just shoved my glass toward him and blurted out, "Rum and Coke."

"And a Long Island." He looked happier when she also ordered. "Put them both on my tab. It's under Josephine."

I turned around to tell her she didn't have to do that, and that I could buy my own drink. Which would have been a real "Brian" move. But she saved me, saying, "You can buy next time. I'm Brilla." And she offered her hand.

"I'm Brian." I shook her slender hand. Touching her sent off nerve bombs in my body. "I thought you were Josephine," I gestured toward the bartender with my head.

"That's my last name. Brilla… Josephine."

"Wow, that's a very pretty name. And you are also very pretty." It sounded so dumb when I said it.

She detected my shyness and said, "Thank you. *You* have an awesome aura."

I thought *I don't normally go for hippie chicks… but in this case, I'll make an exception.*

Our drinks came, and I handed the Long Island Iced Tea to her. She raised her glass in cheers and said, "To us."

I laughed and said, "To us."

We hit it off that evening. I was comfortable talking to her. Jo joined us, and we joked that if the two women got married, my sister would be Josephine Josephine. *Way funnier than Brilla Smith.* Even after having such a good time, I thought that would be the last time I'd see her.

Nate told me that Brilla was, "…out of my league," and I didn't disagree. He wasn't being mean. She really was.

I had her number but didn't call. I second-guessed our interaction, thinking she was probably drunk on LIIT and would never want a guy like me, but the following weekend she was at the bar again and came up to me right away.

"Brian!" She looked happy to see me. "Thanks for not calling me. Work was *crazy* this week, but I was able to focus and get it all done." She pulled out her credit card. "I got the first round." I was stunned by how not calling had worked out. It was like I couldn't do anything wrong.

We started dating and everything evolved so naturally. It was like we were the same person, even though she was this insanely attractive, successful woman with an amazing personality, and I was, well, Brian Smith. *That guy.*

My friends were a little jealous and confused, but Jo wasn't. She said I was a good person and was glad that Brilla could see it.

We tied the knot and only a year later had a daughter, Gabbi. Gabbi has the same crystal clear blue eyes her mother has. When she was six, I took her for her first eye checkup and the doctor reported her vision was perfect, but that her lens was much thinner than normal. She told me that she'd ask around to find out if there were any known long-term effects.

When I mentioned it to Brilla, she said we needed *to talk*.

"Brian, I know you love me. Do you trust me?"

"Of course."

"Do you ever wonder how we ended up together?"

"Yes," I admitted. "You're so perfect compared to me..."

"No. I'm not. Just different. To me you're perfect. But..."

I thought *Oh boy. This is where I get the axe.*

"...Gabbi is better than both of us."

Relieved, I said, "I agree, but I'm not sure where this is going. You said we needed to 'talk.' What about?"

"Sweetie, I'm from another dimension of this world. You can think of it as another planet if that's easier. People evolved similarly, but we're a few millennia ahead. And we've lost some of the physical traits we once had that enabled us to survive. *You* still have those traits, and now Gabbi and Gregory do too."

"Who's Gregory?"

"He's our son," she said, rubbing her firm belly. "I named him Gregory. In my world, it's prophesized that a Gabbi and a Gregory will save our League."

"Your *League*?" The questions were piling up for me. Like *who took Brilla and replaced her with a crazy person?*

"Yes, our species. We call them Leagues. When I said you were perfect, I was referring to your aura. We can see

136

ultra-violet light, and yours is perfect. The optometrist noticed the thin lens on Gabbi's eye. Maybe some other anomalies she didn't mention. Gabbi can see UV light too."

I told Brilla none of this made any sense, and that I thought she might have flipped her lid. She was totally serious, said it like it was scientific fact, but she sounded insane.

"Brian, I can prove it to you. Sort of. I will now disappear for a few seconds and then reappear. I can go between the dimensions. I do it all the time." And then she disappeared.

I was like, *What???* Thinking there was *no way*, and then there was. She came right back.

I started to back away like she was going to kill me and eat me.

"Brian, I know this is way too much information way too fast. But I am concerned that Gabbi's eye doctor results might jeopardize this mission."

"A mission? This is just a mission?" I immediately reverted to my old way of thinking... of course I wasn't good enough to have a real girl this great.

Reading my thoughts, maybe not literally, but *maybe* literally, she said, "Honey, I am not married in my old world. I am yours forever. But we need Gabbi and Greg. We need to try to save our League. If more of us could make the jump it would be easier, but right now I am the only traveler that can procreate. And since humans, here, cannot yet jump, then it's up to me. Greg and Gabbi survived the jump while inside me, but they won't be able to do it on their own for a while. It's only faith in the prophecy that makes me believe they'll be capable one day."

I nodded, still feeling sorry for myself and whatever this was. The future as I had known it before was like a candle that had been snuffed.

Noting my dejection she added, "We're not leaving you now, and we will always be back, but we have other responsibilities as well. I hope you understand."

Of course I didn't. But I wanted to try. Worst case, she was mentally ill and that could be treated. Best case, *she was right*.

Greg was born and showed the expected traits. The three of them enjoyed the paint colors Monet chose after having his right lens extracted. And they all said I had the best aura. We loved each other as a "real family," and I grew to understand their "mission."

Gabbi made the jump at age thirteen, and precocious little Greg a couple years later at age eight. They spent eighty percent of their time with me, in our world, and twenty percent in theirs, preparing their civilization for the future. And they never made me feel like they were out of my League.

THE MAN IN THE DORMER WINDOW

I was in third grade when my parents allowed me to start walking to school. About halfway through the year, I noticed a man in a tall creme-colored house who would watch the kids every day from an arched window just under the roof. He wore the same blue shirt, buttoned to the top, and always had his hands in his pockets, and no expression on his face.

My friends would avoid his house at Halloween, saying he was a pedophile, at best, or, at worst, a murdering psychopath. We never saw him outside; there was no car in the driveway, and he never had visitors.

In fourth grade I started waving at him to see if he would wave back, but he never took his hands out of his pockets. I began to think about him all the time. I wondered how he got groceries, or when he changed his clothes, or if he ever slept. *And why he was always there, watching?* I had to ask him.

One afternoon, on my way home, I made eye contact with him and decided to pay him a visit. I let myself in the gate and marched right up to the door unafraid. I know he could tell I was approaching his house.

I rang the doorbell, waited for a couple of minutes, and then I knocked on the door. I listened against the door, but didn't hear anyone on the other side. I took a peek in the window to see if he was hiding from me, but I didn't see him anywhere. Then I got brave and tried the doorknob. *Locked.* I didn't really expect anything different. I left, somewhat disappointed. He was still up there. I waved but he didn't wave back.

I went back every day that week. I went back every day for a month. One day, the door handle turned. I was excited, not nervous at all, and I went in.

The first floor was like a showroom for furniture. Everything was super clean, like nobody lived there. My house was always a total disaster, even though my mom stayed at home and cleaned all the time.

I called out "Hello," but no one answered. I ventured upstairs. Other than a creak on the third step, the house was absolutely quiet. I started with the room in the front where the man in the blue shirt was most likely to be. I went into the room I thought it was and looked out the window which faced the street. It was made up like a girl's room. It seemed I was in the right place, but the man wasn't there. He must've given me the slip.

I searched all the other rooms, but he was nowhere to be found. Just like on the first floor, it appeared no one lived in the house. All the rooms were very clean: no dust, no pillows or clothes on the floor. I ended up leaving, but I had a plan for the next day.

I told my parents I was going to spend Friday night at Jakob's house. But I actually planned to go to the old man's house to try something different. After school, I repeated the routine from the day before and entered the house. Again, no one was around. After about twenty minutes, I unlocked the *back* door and left loudly out the front. The man was in the window watching me leave.

I took my stuff to Jakob's, but I told him I'd forgotten my comic books, and I'd run home and get them and be back for dinner. I went around the rear of the neighborhood and climbed the old guy's fence. I crept up to his back window and peered in and didn't see him. The back door was still unlocked, and I let myself in.

I listened carefully for any noise. He should have been shuffling about upstairs, but it was silent. I made my way up the stairs, missing the creaky third step and went to the girl's bedroom. I got in the bed and waited. And waited. It started to get dark, and I knew I was late for dinner at Jakob's. I got out of the bed, purposely leaving it a little wrinkled, and shouted, "I know you are in here! Come out and talk! I just want to talk to you." *No response.*

On my way out, I helped myself to a glass of water. I looked in the pantry and the fridge for a snack, but they were both empty. At this point, I started believing he might be a ghost. *Ghosts don't eat. But what ghosts lock and unlock doors?* I was totally confused.

I got back to Jakob's without the comics, and he didn't notice, so I was in the clear after my second B&E that week.

I rode my bike past the house on Saturday after baseball practice and the man was in the window. Then it hit me. *He wasn't in the girl's room. He was one floor higher! He had to be in the attic.* Going into the man's attic sounded a hell of a lot scarier. I didn't even go into *our* attic, but I decided to try after school on Monday.

If anything happened I would get Jakob to call my mom and tell her where I was. But, oddly, I didn't feel threatened. Like the man in the window was playing a game with me, not trying to hurt me. On Monday I stopped by and saw him in the window. The door was unlocked, and I let myself in.

In a closet I thought was a *just* a closet were stairs leading up to another door.

I cracked open the door at the top of the stairs, expecting it to be pitch black, but it was brilliantly lit. The door opened into an enormous room, bigger than my living room and bedroom put together, and at the end of the room in front of the big window was the man in the blue shirt. He was up on a box, and he had no legs.

"You found me. Took you long enough."

And I couldn't stop staring at him. I mean, *he had no legs. How'd he even get up on the box?* I didn't know what to say.

"Cat got your tongue, boy?"

I tried to explain myself. "I see you every day. I wanted to know if you were real, and why you don't wave back."

"Well, I have no arms, obviously." His long, blue sleeves hung limply by his sides. *Seriously, how did he get up on that box?* A toilet flushed and out came a lady, who I expected was his nurse. "This is my nurse, Barbara." *I was right.* "…and my wife."

She greeted me, "Hi, dear, thanks for visiting. Would you like some cookies? We have some in the kitchenette." I just nodded and tried to process the situation.

"I'm Barbara, and you've already met Hal. Hal, did you tell him about your condition?"

"I was about fifty percent done, dear." And he smiled for the first time. "I also have no legs."

No arms, no legs, no shit. I guessed Barbara was the answer to how he got up on the box.

"I like to look out the window most days. It beats lying around in bed... except when we're gettin' it on," he added and winked. Which mystified and weirded me out at the same time.

"What else do you do?"

"Oh, I listen to audiobooks; I watch TV; I eat."

So... normal. I was getting more and more comfortable with the situation. "How did you lose your arms and legs?"

"In the *Wars!*" He pointed with his forehead as he ticked them off. "One arm in World War I, a leg in World War II, another leg in Korea, and another arm in Vietnam."

Whoa! I thought. *He's either a badass or a dumbass.*

"I'm just kidding, kiddo. Birth defect." *That made more sense.* "But it's never held me back. And I met the most wonderful girl fifty-six years ago."

"He's talking about me," Barbara clarified and gave me some cookies and Diet Pepsi. "Hope Diet Pepsi is okay. That's what we like." I thanked her. I drank Diet Pepsi at Jakob's all the time.

"So why do you live in the attic?"

He shrugged. "I can see better up here. And I can't be having Babs carry me up and down the stairs all the time, so we both just live up here."

143

Barbara chimed in, "I tidy up downstairs from time to time, and unlock doors for curious little boys, but most of the time I stay up here with Hal. It's big enough, and we have everything we need. We have a bathroom with a shower, a kitchen, a bed, a TV, lots of light, and a view of the whole neighborhood. It's like a beautiful treehouse."

I was thinking I should move *my* room to the attic too. It was kinda awesome. But I'd been in our attic once, and it was not awesome. It was dark and scary and dirty. It certainly didn't have a bathroom or a kitchen.

I looked at my watch... it had been two hours, and I was almost late for dinner. I hadn't planned on being there more than fifteen minutes. I told them, "Well... I gotta go, but if you need me to get anything for you guys I'd be happy to."

Hal answered, "Thanks for the offer kiddo, but I'd appreciate it if you kept this our little secret. No one knows we're here, and we'd prefer to keep it that way. A couple of old defenseless folks like us might get robbed."

I promised I wouldn't tell anyone, even my parents. Barbara gave me a spare key, so she could keep the door locked, and invited me to come back anytime I'd like, as long as it was during daylight.

I visited the Johnsons almost every week for years. They told me they used to have a daughter named Grace, but she died of leukemia when she was only twenty. They also told me I was like a son to them, and I considered them my second set of parents.

When I got a car, I drove by every morning and waved to Hal on my way to school. But one Monday, Hal was not in his window. I thought maybe I'd just missed him... that had happened only two or three times ever, and it usually meant he was in the bathroom. But the next day he wasn't there either. Thinking something might be up, I stopped by after school.

Climbing the stairs, a rotten odor got stronger, and when I opened the attic door, I found out what it was. Barbara was dead on the bed with her eyes and mouth open, and Hal was nowhere in sight. I called out for him, and he groaned from the floor on the other side of the bed.

He was bruised and bleeding from repeated self-inflicted blows to his head. I grabbed him and put him on the bed next to Barbara. He immediately rolled over using his neck and started kissing her and saying he was, "So sorry, so sorry."

He was barely coherent, but it sounded like, "You have to let me finish the job. I need to die and be with her." He managed to convey that Barabara had suffered a heart attack on Saturday afternoon when he was at the window, and he couldn't get to her on the bed or dial 911 the past three days. So, he tried to take his own life, trying to bludgeon himself on the bottom corner of the nightstand and apparently several other pieces of furniture, as evidenced from the blood trails.

By then I was an accomplice, having moved him to the bed. He begged me to finish him off, and then I could move him back to the bed and tell the police everything. I was torn, but I decided to let him have his wish.

I jostled the nightstand and the lamp with a metal base resembling an "X" *happened* to land on the floor. As I placed Hal back on the floor, he said, "We loved you Greg," and then he impaled his neck into the spiky lamp stand. I sobbed as he died in minutes. People like the Johnsons deserved better. After I was sure he was dead, I put him back on the bed next to Barbara and called 911. I placed a blanket over their bodies and waited downstairs for the cops to come.

Because I moved the body, I was under suspicion, but the police allowed me to stay with my family while they processed the evidence, and after the autopsies, they cleared me.

Unexpectedly, the Johnsons left their house to *me*. I rented it out to help pay for college, and now that I have a job nearby, I'm moving in. I'm going to live up here in the attic for a while. It just feels right.

And now I'm looking out over the neighborhood, with my hands in my pockets, remembering the kindest and coolest people I ever met, hoping I will grow up to be just like them.

SWEET MEMORIES

In June of 1998, I visited Grandma Winnie at her house outside Tulsa, Oklahoma. It'd been four months since Grandpa K died. I wanted to make the short trip from Norman earlier, but I had a tough semester: I didn't even leave the campus for Spring Break.

My dad's parents both passed away when my sister and I were very young, so Grandma Winnie and Grandpa K were the only "old people" we knew. Growing up, we'd go to their house for Thanksgiving, for the week after Christmas, and for a couple of weeks each summer.

Grandma would bake cookies and cakes and liked to crochet and watch football. Grandpa smoked fat cigars and would drive us into town for milkshakes at Hank's.

Grandpa used to be a mechanic and tinkered with old cars in the shed next to his house. Grandma found him dead under his 1978 Lil' Red Express pick-up truck that looked like a bad-ass Hot Wheels car. He'd suffered a major heart attack, and at 72 years old and 350 pounds, we weren't surprised, just sad. He was a nice grandpa.

Grandpa and Grandma asked to be cremated and spread on the land at their house. I would have thought they'd want to be buried at a cemetery, but they said the house held sweet memories for them, and they wanted to stay there forever. And they didn't want some housing development to dig them up in fifty years... at least that's what Grandma told me when I asked her during my visit.

She had recovered from the initial shock of losing the love of her life, and she was starting to return to her old hobbies. She even had a computer and was learning how to use e-mail.

I found her at the desk with her hand on the mouse, but she wasn't doing anything. Not reading the screen, just staring past the monitor into space. I asked if she needed help with something, and she didn't respond. She was far away, deep in thought. I decided not to bother her... she was breathing... so I crossed the kitchen to grab a cookie from the counter.

"Oh, hi, Liam. I must have zoned out. That's what you kids say, right? Zoned out?"

"Yep, that's right, Grandma. I didn't want to disturb you."

"I was just thinking about your grandpa. I swear I could smell his aftershave, and it took me to another place. Sometimes that happens when you're with someone for fifty years."

I understood where she was coming from even though I had no way to identify, being just nineteen at the time. But she was happy, so I figured it was a good thing.

I planned to stay at Grandma's for a week before meeting up with my old friends to go tubing. She asked me to take a look at Grandpa's old cars and recommend what we should do with them. She wanted to turn the garage into a place to do crafting and to store some of her materials and finished products. She was going to learn how to sell them on the internet. *Wow.*

I was working in the shed, sweating my ass off, inventorying the loose parts that hadn't made it into Lil'

Red, when Grandma appeared in the doorway with lemonade. I gulped it down like a small fish trying to swallow the ocean. She poured me a second glass and told me not to drink it so fast, and to come inside if it got too hot.

I resumed my work, and, curious where Grandpa left off, I got under the car. I could have sworn he was under there with me. I detected the odors of his cigars and sweat. *We were working on the car together.* Before I knew it, Grandma reappeared in the doorway to announce dinner. I'm not sure I recorded a thing in my log, but nevertheless, I had a productive afternoon, spending lost time with Grandpa K.

Throughout the week I had more feelings Grandpa K was haunting his old place. I swear I could smell his aftershave and the whisky he drank most evenings. I mentioned it to Grandma, and she said, "Yes, dear, my Gus is still with us."

I found her several more times in that trancelike state, enraptured, and I tried not to disturb her when she was having one of her episodes.

I was back in the garage, my task almost done, when Grandma appeared out of nowhere, like a ghost. I hadn't heard her come in, but she was watching me, curiously. I wondered if *I* had awoken from a trance like hers. Grandma didn't say anything, just took my half-eaten lunch, smiled, and went back into the house.

Friday came, and I left for Tahlequah to meet up with my friends. I felt Grandpa was in the car with me for the hour's drive. I was sure the scent from their house was in my clothes. *Good thing we'd be in swimsuits all weekend.* But even when we were floating down the river, it was as if Grandpa K was floating with us.

One night, as we were drinking beer, my friend Jake said he was craving cigars. He thought someone on the river was smoking one, so he went into town and bought a box of them for us.

We had never smoked before, but we were all going to different colleges and growing up, and I guessed that was something Jake did now. When he came back with my Grandpa's brand of cigars, out of all the possible choices, I freaked. *Grandpa's ghost was there on the road trip with us.* I told the guys about the coincidence, and we all toasted Grandpa K. It was like we were making a great memory with him even after he was gone.

I didn't need to go through Tulsa on my way back to OK City, but I did. I had completed everything before the tubing weekend, but I was drawn to return. Grandpa wasn't riding shotgun this time. *Maybe he wanted to stay by the river a while longer.*

When I pulled up to Grandma's house, a car was parked on the gravel drive. I wasn't sure if I should go in, as she wasn't expecting me, but I did anyway. A man from the Social Security Administration was meeting with Grandma, going over Grandpa's transfer of benefits. The agent introduced himself as Arthur Miller. I'm usually terrible with names, but I remembered because I had written a paper on the playwright Arthur Miller in English Lit class the previous semester.

This Arthur Miller was quite personable, and, though the IRS doesn't normally make house calls, he lived only a half-mile away and was happy to drop in. He was also a recent widower, so they had something in common.

As he got into his car, Arthur told me Grandma was, "sharp as a tack."

"She understood everything immediately and I never had to repeat myself. In my line of work, that's rare. And how she loved her husband, Gus… I could see it in her eyes, you know? She says that Gus is still with us. And I think I believe her." With that Arthur pulled out of the driveway and headed down the road to his nearby house, done for the day.

I spent the rest of the week out at Grandma's house. And Grandpa came back from Tahlequah, the cigar-smell with him, and the three of us were together again.

Uncharacteristically, I went into town and bought a used copy of Arthur Miller's *The Crucible* to read for *fun* when *Arthur Miller 2.0* stopped by. He brought the family cookbook they discussed during his first visit. I let Grandma and her new neighbor get to know each other as I read my book. They drank lemonade, had a piece of apple pie, and picked out which recipes to try.

I left at the end of the week and Grandpa lingered with me for a while, but eventually, I was back in my routine, hanging out with old friends. I guess Grandma and Arthur grew sweet on each other, because Grandma would email me all the time telling me how it was nice to have *AM2* (my new nickname for him) around and how he was a perfect gentleman, "…just like your grandpa."

Mom asked me who this guy was that Grandma was so smitten by. She was anxious about her mom moving on so quickly, and was worried about AM2's intentions, but I vouched for him, telling her I approved. We had discussed the ghost of Grandpa K. Maybe having Arthur would encourage Grandma to move on.

I visited them once more at the end of August as school was about to restart. Something about the country house made me want to return. Arthur stopped by and was smoking Grandpa's cigar brand now. I asked Grandma if she had given him Grandpa's old cigars and she said, "No dear, he bought them all by himself. I think it's wonderful. I love the smell."

I straight-out asked if they were dating, and she said, "I like having him around, that's all." And then something weird, "He's okay with Gus still being here."

I was hoping this new flame would push Gus firmly into the afterlife, but after several days I was sure Grandma was right. Gus *was* still around. Grandma would go into her trances, and I woke from one myself, Arthur asking me if I wanted anything from town. Half-dazed, I told him, "You know, sometimes I think my Grandpa is still here." And he said, "Yep, I do too."

I said, "He was kinda sweaty and smelly with the cigars and the whiskey. I think the house might need a new coat of paint."

AM2 seemed relieved he had someone to confide in. "I think I'm actually *becoming* him. I'm not sure why I started smoking cigars. And I bought the same aftershave your grandpa used to use. I think it's *very* strange, but... it kinda feels right... and I think Winnie likes it."

He called her Winnie, which made sense. They were definitely an item, joined by some mysterious ex-husband, ghost matchmaker. I laughed at the thought. If Grandpa K were here, I think he'd either punch Arthur's lights out or laugh too.

The night before I was to return to school, I wandered into the kitchen for a glass of water. Grandma was at the counter. I thought she'd already gone to bed. She seemed to be in a trance—*maybe sleepwalking*?

She was making lemonade, as she had thousands of times, so that wasn't strange. What *was* strange was that Grandpa's urn was on the counter. She had moved it from the mantle, next to the pitcher of water and the sugar and the freshly squeezed and strained lemons—along with the long spoon she used to stir the lemonade.

She removed the lid off the urn, took the long stirring spoon, and dipped it inside, scooping a level spoonful before adding it to the pitcher. As the water turned slightly cloudy, my memory became clear—so many glasses of lemonade. Gulping it down in the garage, my half-eaten lunch beside me. Arthur sipping over his cookbook. The smell of Grandpa in my pores, lingering for days.

He was inside me, not just in spirit. *Inside. Me.* I threw up in the sink.

I roused Grandma from her trance and asked her what she was doing. She covered her mouth, saying, "Oh my! What have I done?" Like it was the first time.

As I coaxed her shaky hand to spread the remaining ashes in the yard, I could tell she had been trying to hold on to memories in the only way she knew how. Sweetened with a little sugar, and lemon.

Letting go would be hard. But she had Arthur, aka *Grandpa K 2.0*, and with him, the smells and memories of Gus would remain close at hand.

JULIE

"…and when you're done with Julie, throw her in the kiln."

I was almost finished mapping Julie's face when my boss, Dr. Zydros, informed me that we wouldn't be doing further experiments with her. She was the tenth in a series of twenty-five test cases altering nasal dimensions in Caucasian females.

From a single model, Eve, we manipulated DNA to see how changes manifested themselves empirically. Each subject was grown from scratch, accelerated through protein delivery from a fetus to an adult in just under twenty-seven months. Currently, we were only interested in facial features, so the bodies were discarded at three months, and the heads were grown via heart-lung machines. The brain growth was chemically stunted in the areas of pain, self-awareness, and emotion, so the subjects were unaware of their surroundings or purpose, despite being quite alive.

When I first began working for Dr. Zydros, I had been seeking a change from working in an organ farm, growing ears and noses for transplants. Despite the threat of our company being shut down for unethical practices, I had taken this challenge to further my career. I didn't consider the full living heads in the office anything more than lab experiments. Until Julie.

When I saw Julie move into her final maturity level, I was smitten. Something about the width of her nasal passages made my heart do flips. She wasn't much different from subject Anna or even Hallie at first glance, but upon clearer inspection, she was like the baby bear's bed in Goldilocks... *just right*.

Of course, there was no chance of an actual relationship with her. I had my own living, breathing, talking girl at home, Jennifer, who I was about to marry in the next few weeks. But somehow, I wanted to save Julie, preserve her from the eventual destruction in the kiln.

We stored a fair number of heads, after initial measurements to assess advanced aging or to spawn variants, and I told Dr. Zydros that Julie was an ideal candidate as she exhibited the mean value and could be used as a baseline for derivative experiments. He shunned my proposal, saying he sought extraordinary specimens, not average ones. His definition of "extraordinary" seemed capricious and perhaps opposed to mine.

I wasn't sure that if I defied him and kept Julie in the storage vault he would even notice, but I didn't want to risk being fired over a breach of protocol. So, I disconnected her and snuck her home in a lined backpack.

That weekend, I preserved her using techniques learned from my previous job, enclosed her in a high-vacuum bell jar, and placed her in the fridge. My shed doubled as a research room, and Jennifer only ventured in for office supplies or if she needed to look up warranties or medical records in our filing cabinet. If she stumbled upon Julie, I would just say I was bringing work home, and then I'd have to make other arrangements.

Jennifer and I were wed as planned and spent a week in St. Lucia. I only thought about Julie maybe fifteen or twenty times. Of course, she was dead now, but she still held a place in my heart alongside Jennifer. Once we returned home, I was happily reunited, and life continued as normal. Until the day Jennifer phoned me at work.

"There's a woman's head in your fridge!" She was screaming at me over the phone. I stepped outside and told her my well-rehearsed, "It's just a work experiment, honey. I have a few measurements to do, and then it will be gone. Just leave it alone."

"I knew you did weird shit at work," she replied, "but not *that* weird. I want it *gone* by this weekend. Get it back to the lab or whatever you do with those things when you're done."

"Will do. Sorry, babe." And I hung up. So now I had to enact Plan B, which involved paying cash for offsite refrigerated storage, usually reserved for people's wine collections.

However, when I walked through the doorway, Jennifer had moved Julie to the middle of the kitchen table and was just sitting with her. Like they were friends having a conversation. I shook my head and started toward the bell jar when Jennifer stopped me. "Hold on. Sit down."

I sat.

"I might have overreacted earlier." I looked at Jennifer quizzically. "There's something beautiful about her. Isn't there?"

Knowing this was most likely a trap, I feigned indifference, "From what I can tell she's perfectly average."

Jennifer drew in toward Julie a few inches studying her intently. "Maybe... that's what it is.... She's *perfectly* average." Jennifer appeared genuinely interested in Julie. "I can't take my eyes off of her."

Keeping with my narrative, I said, "I was so far behind I broke protocol to bring her here so I could finish, but I have to get her back and submit the report."

"What if we kept her?"

I was taken aback. Dumbfounded. "Here? Like... forever?"

"Yes, like *forever*. She would be our secret. Until we have kids, then she'll have to go. Probably."

I continued to play dumb, but inside my heart was flipping... for both of my girls. "I can sign off that I disposed of her, and they might never know. But if I get caught, I might get fired."

"Honey. I don't want you to lose your job, but if we can, let's keep her. She's... exciting."

So, I faked that I turned in my report and told Jennifer we were in the clear. It's now a year and a half later. We have a new fridge, hidden in a secret room behind our living room bookshelf.

And we also have Jackie.

And Jordan.

FREEDOM ROAD

Sometimes I must escape the closeness of the city. Mumbai is the City of Dreams, but it seems everyone dreams of sitting in each other's lap.

Every Saturday morning before dawn, I head out on my Interceptor toward Pune. The roads are empty. At this hour, on this day, not many people drive into town or out of it. It's a peaceful, relaxing feeling, like I am the only person in the world.

One such Saturday morning, I left my chawl under cover of darkness. I recall sweltering humidity, with no air circulating in from the sea, but luckily, after living my whole life here, I can breathe water.

A dog barked somewhere off, but otherwise, the neighborhood slept. I remember thinking something was different. Maybe the barometric pressure was muffling the sounds of the city, which, at 5 a.m. should have already been stirring. Sometimes I listen to music when I travel, but on this morning, the bike's reassuring purr was all I wanted.

As I crossed Thane Creek into Navi Mumbai, I passed a few motorists traveling into town, headed toward early morning shifts. This indication of humanity usually persists until I reach Dheku, then, pure freedom. Even if another vehicle appears, I block them out. Just me and my bike.

At dawn, as I emerged from the Khandala Ghat, I lowered my dark visor to block the rising sun ahead. Instead, an even more intense burst of light hit from all directions. It lasted three or four seconds, then everything returned to normal. Disoriented, I pulled over to the side of the road.

Raising my visor, everything appeared as expected, and I wondered if I had just had a stroke. One time, when I was working at my uncle's farm, I became so dehydrated the field and the house turned white, and I passed out. But this was different. I wasn't sick, only confused.

I remounted my bike and drove on through Lonavala not seeing a single soul. Not even a stray dog or a cow. Like when we were in lockdown for the coronavirus in 2021, but even creepier. I recalled childhood stories of ghosts haunting this highway, but now I was thinking *even the ghosts are hiding*.

Typically, I will stop in Lonavala at Kumar's to decide whether to continue to Pune or head back to Mumbai. Their Kanda Poha is the best, and it sets my course for the rest of the day. But Kumar's looked closed, and so did the petrol station, so I rode on toward Pune.

I visit friends north of the city every few months, but the whole goal of my Saturday trips is to avoid the hustle and bustle, so I usually turn around when I hit NH48. Given I hadn't seen a person since the light flash, I kept going into the city. Maybe I was looking for another person who, like me, hadn't gotten the memo to stay inside.

Pune is a big town, with five million people, or more, but twenty miles outside it was deserted. Christians have a belief in "The Rapture," an event where they believe they will instantly transfer from Earth to Heaven. Maybe The Rapture didn't care if you were Christian or Hindu, Islamic or Buddhist, or nothing. Maybe it didn't matter who you were as long as you weren't... *me.*

I rode into an abandoned city. Cars were stopped in the streets with no drivers. The people weren't hiding; they were gone.

I started to panic and tried my mobile. No signal. I shouted out, "Hello!" expecting to hear a haunting echo, but it died a few feet from me, sounding small and ineffective. I hopped on my bike and went to a gas station for a refill. Bharat has self-serve, and the pumps still worked. No one was there to take my money, so I left, feeling a little guilty about not paying.

I zipped all over Pune, heading to my friends' flats in a hi-rise near Pune University in the northwest part of town. I parked out front, let myself in the lobby, took the lift to the eighteenth floor, and knocked on their door. No answer. I went down the hall trying doors until one opened. I called out to the lukewarm chai left on the counter.

A computer sat on a small desk in the corner, powered on and unlocked.

What I saw on the internet shocked me. People were missing from all over India and South Asia. Planes landed at empty airports in Dubai, Dhaka, and Islamabad. Empty planes had fallen from local skies.

No one had made contact anywhere inside India, or in the surrounding countries. So why me?

I reached out on a live video stream, and, within minutes, I had hundreds of thousands of viewers. Then my chat went blank. I was about to start a new one when I got a private message asking me to join a session. Hoping for rescue, I was suddenly in front of an impressive group of military and political leaders from around the globe.

I recounted my story, including the flash of light at the Khandala Ghat. People were scurrying in the background and a woman was pointing to a map. I had confirmed what they suspected. I was at the exact epicenter of whatever had gone on. Within a 2200 km radius from that point, no living beings existed. They had no explanation, but were deploying a rescue team to the Pune airport, and asked me to meet them in four hours.

I sat in the flat and reflected on my fortune. Being in the right place at the right time. Or, if it was the glorious Rapture, maybe the wrong place.

My social media accounts were still exploding with comments, and I got an idea. I renamed myself GhostofMumbai and posted a video. Within the hour I already had enough followers to monetize the accounts. I hit the road with a backpack of snacks from the kitchen and headed south. Opposite from the direction of the airport.

I would have my Saturday of freedom extend as long as possible before being detained and poked and prodded. Over the next two weeks, I posted videos from random towns, staying just a hair ahead of international agencies trying to scoop me up. They threatened to take down my posts, but they didn't. They needed them to track me.

They froze my bank account, but I didn't need money. I had unlimited fuel and stayed in pleasant accommodations. I expected to see police cars around every bend and considered upgrading to a faster ride—but my bike was a part of me now. We had survived the Rapture together.

After evading arrest for seventeen days, I agreed to surrender on three conditions. One, indemnity for trespassing and other small crimes during my spree, two, I could return to India anytime, and three, I could keep the funds I earned as GhostofMumbai.

It worked out better than I thought. The media blitz was unreal, and I was elevated to some type of god status by people around the world, but especially from India... Chosen One, et cetera. But all this attention, all these people, it wasn't me. I moved back to an isolated India. And millions of Indians from all over the world followed.

I am the newly elected President of the Republic. Together, we are rebuilding the City of Dreams and our country. But every Saturday, I still disappear to find a lonely trail—just me and my bike, to feel as if I'm the only person left in the world.

Dear Reader,

Thank you so much for reading Hope In One Hand.... Did you enjoy it?

If you did, please consider leaving me a review. I would love to hear what you have to say and your review may drive more readership.

Please check out the individual story cover art on the last page and visit www.phillbradley.com for additional stories and updates.

Best regards,

Phill

INSIDERS

Would you like the chance to read stories from the next collection early?

Find out when the next collection is out?

Use the QR code below to be an insider and **get one bonus story for joining***

* Totally free - just need a name and valid email address

BETA READERS

When joining the Insiders mailing list, you can indicate if you are interested in joining the Beta Reader Program. Spots are limited, but I will let you know if you are accepted. Beta Readers have access to most new works before they are published.

More on the Beta Reader program can be found at www.phillbradley.com.

Club Cemetery
Phill Bradley

HOPE IN ONE HAND...

THE COVERS

FINDING COMFORT

PHILL BRADLEY

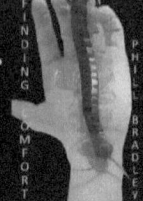

Fishplace

Phill Bradley

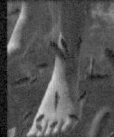

FREEDOM ROAD

PHILL BRADLEY

HEAVEN'S ON THE OTHER SIDE OF A CHAIN LINK FENCE

PHILL BRADLEY

HOPPERS of HOPPERS

PHILL BRADLEY

Hotel Black

Phill Bradley

Julie

Phill Bradley

Kolbolsokh
Phill Bradley

KISS MYSELF

PHILL BRADLEY

Little Red Wagon

Phill Bradley

MARY NICHOLS HIGHWAY

PHILL BRADLEY

OUT OF HER LEAGUE

PHILL BRADLEY

NOW

PHILL BRADLEY

SOUL-LETTING

PHILL BRADLEY

SPIDERMEN

PHILL BRADLEY

Sweet Memories

Phill Bradley

THE ALIENS THAT SMILED BACK

PHILL BRADLEY

THE HEDGE

PHILL BRADLEY

THE MAN IN THE CORNER

PHILL BRADLEY

THIN SKIN

PHILL BRADLEY

TUNNELS IN 2D

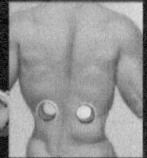

PHILL BRADLEY

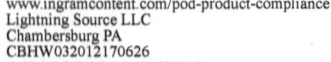